One eyebrow spiked. 'You seem so confident I'm going to hand myself to you on a silver platter. Isn't that a tad foolish?'

There was that tone again—the one that said she didn't believe him. That she thought this was some sort of twisted game on his part.

'I guess we'll find out one way or the other when the sordid details are laid out for you on Monday. All you need to concern yourself about today is picking out an engagement ring that makes the right statement.'

Eva's striking green eyes clashed with his and that lightning bolt struck again. 'And what statement would that be?' she challenged.

Zaccheo let loose the chilling half-smile that he knew made his enemies quake. 'Why, that you belong to me, of course.'

Seven Sexy Sins

The true *taste of temptation!*

From greed to gluttony, lust to envy,
these fabulous stories explore what seven sexy sins
mean in the twenty-first century!

Whether pride goes before a fall, or wrath leads to
a passion that consumes entirely, one thing is certain:
the road to true love has never been more enticing!

So you decide:

How can it be a sin when it feels so good?

Sloth—Cathy Williams

Lust—Dani Collins

Pride—Kim Lawrence

Gluttony—Maggie Cox

Greed—Sara Craven

Wrath—Maya Blake

Envy—Annie West

Seven titles by some of
Mills & Boon Modern Romance's
most treasured and exciting authors!

A MARRIAGE
FIT FOR A SINNER

BY
MAYA BLAKE

First published in Great Britain 2015
by Mills & Boon, an imprint of Harlequin (UK) Limited,
Eton House, 18-24 Paradise Road, Richmond, Surrey, TW9 1SR

© 2015 Maya Blake

ISBN: 978-0-263-25913-1

Harlequin (UK) Limited's policy is to use papers that are natural,
renewable and recyclable products and made from wood grown in
sustainable forests. The logging and manufacturing processes conform
to the legal environmental regulations of the country of origin.

Printed and bound in Great Britain
by CPI Antony Rowe, Chippenham, Wiltshire

Maya Blake's hopes of becoming a writer were born when she picked up her first romance aged thirteen. Little did she know her dream would come true! Does she still pinch herself every now and then, to make sure it's not a dream? Yes, she does!

Feel free to pinch her too, via Twitter, Facebook or Goodreads! Happy reading!

Books by Maya Blake

Mills & Boon Modern Romance

Married for the Prince's Convenience
Innocent in His Diamonds
His Ultimate Prize
Marriage Made of Secrets
The Sinful Art of Revenge
The Price of Success

The Untameable Greeks

What the Greek's Money Can't Buy
What the Greek Can't Resist
What the Greek Wants Most

The 21st Century Gentleman's Club

The Ultimate Playboy

In December 2015 look out for *Brunetti's Secret Son* featuring Romeo from *A Marriage Fit for a Sinner*

Visit the Author Profile page
at millsandboon.co.uk for more titles.

CHAPTER ONE

'ONE PLATINUM CHRONOGRAPH WATCH. A pair of diamond-studded cufflinks. Gold signet ring. Six hundred and twenty-five pounds cash, and…Obsidian Privilege Card. Right, I think that's everything, sir. Sign here to confirm return of your property.'

Zaccheo Giordano didn't react to the warden's sneer as he scrawled on the barely legible form. Nor did he react to the resentful envy in the man's eyes when his gaze drifted to where the sleek silver limousine waited beyond three sets of barbed wire.

Romeo Brunetti, Zaccheo's second-in-command and the only person he would consider draping the term *friend* upon, stood beside the car, brooding and unsmiling, totally unruffled by the armed guard at the gate or the bleak South East England surroundings.

Had Zaccheo been in an accommodating mood, he'd have cracked a smile.

But he wasn't in an accommodating mood. He hadn't been for a very long time. Fourteen months, two weeks, four days and nine hours to be exact. Zaccheo was positive he could count down to the last second if required.

No one would require it of him, of course. He'd served his time. With three and a half months knocked off his eighteen-month sentence *for good behaviour.*

The rage fused into his DNA bubbled beneath his skin. He showed no outward sign of it as he pocketed his belongings. The three-piece Savile Row suit he'd entered prison in stank of decay and misery, but Zaccheo didn't care.

He'd never been a slave to material comforts. His need for validation went far deeper. The need to elevate himself into a better place had been a soul-deep pursuit from the moment he was old enough to recognise the reality of the life he'd been born into. A life that had been a never-ending whirlpool of humiliation, violence and greed. A life that had seen his father debased and dead at thirty-five.

Memories tumbled like dominoes as he walked down the harshly lit corridor to freedom. He willed the overwhelming sense of injustice that had festered for long, harrowing months not to explode from his pores.

The doors clanged shut behind him.

Zaccheo froze, then took his first lungful of free air with fists clenched and eyes shut. He absorbed the sound of birds chirping in the late-winter morning sun, listened to the distant rumble of the motorway as he'd done many nights from his prison cell.

Opening his eyes, he headed towards the fifteen-foot gate. A minute later, he was outside.

'Zaccheo, it's good to see you again,' Romeo said gravely, his eyes narrowing as he took him in.

Zaccheo knew he looked a sight. He hadn't bothered with a razor blade or a barber's clippers in the last three months and he'd barely eaten once he'd unearthed the truth behind his incarceration. But he'd spent a lot of time in the prison gym. It'd been that or go mad with the clawing hunger for retribution.

He shrugged off his friend's concern and moved to the open door.

'Did you bring what I asked for?' he asked.

Romeo nodded. '*Sì*. All three files are on the laptop.'

Zaccheo slid onto the plush leather seat. Romeo slid in next to him and poured them two glasses of Italian-made cognac.

'*Salute,*' Romeo muttered.

Zaccheo took the drink without responding, threw back the amber liquid and allowed the scent of power and affluence—the tools he'd need for his plan to succeed—to wash over him.

As the low hum of the luxury engine whisked him away from the place he'd been forced to call home for over a year, Zaccheo reached for the laptop.

Icy rage trembled through his fingers as the Giordano Worldwide Inc. logo flickered to life. His life's work, almost decimated through another's greed and lust for power. It was only with Romeo's help that GWI hadn't gone under in the months after Zaccheo had been sent to prison for a crime he didn't commit. He drew quiet satisfaction that not only had GWI survived—thanks to Romeo—it had thrived.

But his personal reputation had not.

He was out now. Free to bring those culpable to justice. He didn't plan on resting until every last person responsible for attempting to destroy his life paid with the destruction of theirs.

Shaking out his hand to rid it of its tremble, he hit the Open key.

The information was thorough although Zaccheo knew most of its contents. For three months he'd checked and double-checked his sources, made sure every detail was nailed down tight.

He exhaled at the first picture that filled his screen.

Oscar Pennington III. Distant relative to the royal family. Etonian. Old, if spent, money. Very much part of the establishment. Greedy. Indiscriminate. His waning property portfolio had received a much-needed injection of capital exactly fourteen months and two weeks ago when he'd become sole owner of London's most talked about building—The Spire.

Zaccheo swallowed the savage growl that rumbled from his soul. Icily calm, he flicked through pages of Pennington celebrating his revived success with galas, lavish dinner parties and polo tournaments thrown about like confetti. One picture showed him laughing with one of his two children.

Sophie Pennington. Private education all the way to finishing school. Classically beautiful. Ball-breaker. She'd proven beyond a doubt that she had every intention of becoming Oscar's carbon copy.

Grimly, he closed her file and moved to the last one.

Eva Pennington.

This time the growl couldn't be contained. Nor could he stem the renewed shaking in his hand as he clicked her file.

Caramel-blonde hair tumbled down her shoulders in thick, wild waves. Dark eyebrows and lashes framed moss-green eyes, accentuated dramatically with black eyeliner. Those eyes had gripped his attention with more force than he'd been comfortable with the first time he'd looked into them. As had the full, bow-shaped lips currently curved in a smouldering smile. His screen displayed a head-and-shoulders shot, but the rest of Eva Pennington's body was imprinted indelibly on Zaccheo's mind. He didn't struggle to recall the petite, curvy shape, or that she forced herself to wear heels even though she hated them, in order to make herself taller.

He certainly didn't struggle to recall her individual atrocity. He'd lain in his prison bed condemning himself for being astounded by her singular betrayal, when the failings of both his parents and his dealings with the *establishment* should've taught him better. He'd prided himself on reading between the lines to spot schemers and gold-diggers ten miles away. Yet he'd been fooled.

The time he'd wasted on useless bitterness was the most excruciating of all; time he would gladly claw back if he could.

Firming his lips, he clicked through the pages, running through her life for the past year and a half. At the final page, he froze.

'How new is this last information?'

'I added that to the file yesterday. I thought you'd want to know,' Romeo replied.

Zaccheo stared at the newspaper clipping, shock waves rolling through him. *'Sì, grazie...'*

'Do you wish to return to the Esher estate or the penthouse?' Romeo asked.

Zaccheo read the announcement again, taking in pertinent details. Pennington Manor. Eight o'clock. Three hundred guests. Followed by an intimate family dinner on Sunday at The Spire.

The Spire...the building that should've been Zaccheo's greatest achievement.

'The estate,' he replied. It was closer.

He closed the file as Romeo instructed the driver.

Relaxing against the headrest, Zaccheo tried to let the hum of the engine soothe him. But it was no use. He was far from calm.

He'd have to alter his plan. Not that it mattered too much in the long run.

A chain is only as strong as its weakest link. While all three Penningtons had colluded in his incarceration, this new information demanded he use a different tactic, one he'd first contemplated and abandoned. Either way, Zaccheo didn't plan to rest until all of them were stripped of what they cherished most—their wealth and affluence.

He'd intended to wait a day or two to ensure he had Oscar Pennington where he wanted him before he struck. That plan was no longer viable.

Bringing down the family who'd framed him for criminal negligence couldn't wait till Monday.

His first order of business would be tackled *tonight*.

Starting with the youngest member of the family—Eva Pennington.

His ex-fiancée.

Eva Pennington stared at the dress in her sister's hand. 'Seriously? There's no way I'm wearing that. Why didn't you tell me the clothes I left behind had been given away?'

'Because you said you didn't want them when you moved out. Besides, they were old and out of fashion. I had *this* couriered from New York this morning. It's the latest couture and on loan to us for twenty-four hours,' Sophie replied.

Eva pursed her lips. 'I don't care if it was woven by ten thousand silk worms. I'm not wearing a dress that makes me look like a gold-digger *and* a slut. And considering the state of our finances, I'd have thought you'd be more careful what you splashed money on.' She couldn't stem her bewilderment as to why Sophie and her father blithely ignored the fact that money was extremely tight.

Sophie huffed. 'This is a one-of-a-kind dress, and, unless I'm mistaken, it's the kind of dress your future husband likes his women to wear. Anyway, you'll be out of it in less than four hours, once the right photographs have been taken, and the party's over.'

Eva gritted her teeth. 'Stop trying to manage me, Sophie. You're forgetting who pulled this bailout together. If I hadn't come to an agreement with Harry, we'd have been sunk come next week. As to what he likes his women to wear, if you'd bothered to speak to me first I'd have saved you the trouble of going to unnecessary expense. I dress for myself and no one else.'

'Speak to you first? When you and Father neglected to afford me the same courtesy before you hatched this plan behind my back?' Sophie griped.

Eva's heart twisted at the blatant jealousy in her sister's voice.

As if it weren't enough that the decision she'd spent the past two weeks agonising over still made her insides clench in horror. It didn't matter that the man she'd agreed to marry was her friend and she was helping him as much as he was helping her. Marriage was a step she'd rather not have taken.

It was clear, however, her sister didn't see it that way. Sophie's escalating discontentment at any relationship Eva tried to forge with their father was part of the reason Eva had moved out of Pennington Manor. Not that their father was an easy man to live with.

For as long as she could remember, Sophie had been possessive of their father's attention. While their mother had been alive, it'd been bearable and easier to accept that Sophie was their father's preferred child, while Eva was her mother's, despite wanting to be loved equally by both parents.

After their mother's death, every interaction Eva had tried to have with their father had been met with bristling confrontation from Sophie, and indifference from their father.

But, irrational as it was, it didn't stop Eva from trying to reason with the sister she'd once looked up to.

'We didn't go behind your back. You were away on a business trip—'

'Trying to use the business degree that doesn't seem to mean anything any more. Not when *you* can swoop in after three years of performing tired ballads in seedy pubs to save the day,' Sophie interjected harshly.

Eva hung on to her temper by a thread, but pain stung deep at the blithe dismissal of her passion. 'You know I resigned from Penningtons because Father only hired me so I could attract a suitable husband. And just because my dreams don't coincide with yours—'

'That's just it. You're twenty-four and still *dreaming*. The rest of us don't have that luxury. And we certainly don't land on our feet by clicking our fingers and having a millionaire solve all our problems.'

'Harry is saving *all of us*. And you really think I've *landed on my feet* by getting engaged for the second time in two years?' Eva asked.

Sophie dropped the offensive dress on Eva's bed. 'To everyone who matters, this is your first engagement. The other one barely lasted five minutes. Hardly anyone knows it happened.'

Hurt-laced anger swirled through her veins. '*I* know it happened.'

'If my opinion matters around here any more, then I suggest you don't broadcast it. It's a subject best left in the past, just like the man it involved.'

Pain stung deeper. 'I can't pretend it didn't happen because of what occurred afterwards.'

'The last thing we need right now is any hint of scandal. And I don't know why you're blaming Father for what happened when you should be thanking him for extricating you from that man before it was too late,' Sophie defended heatedly.

That man.

Zaccheo Giordano.

Eva wasn't sure whether the ache lodged beneath her ribs came from thinking about him or from the reminder of how gullible she'd been to think he was any different from every other man who'd crossed her path.

She relaxed her fists when they balled again.

This was why she preferred her life away from their family home deep in the heart of Surrey.

It was why her waitress colleagues knew her as Eva Penn, a hostess at Siren, the London nightclub where she also sang part-time, instead of Lady Eva Pennington, daughter of Lord Pennington.

Her relationship with her father had always been difficult, but she'd never thought she'd lose her sister so completely, too.

She cleared her throat. 'Sophie, this agreement with Harry wasn't supposed to undermine anything you were doing with Father to save Penningtons. There's no need to be upset or jealous. I'm not trying to take your place—'

'Jealous! Don't be ridiculous,' Sophie sneered, although the trace of panic in her voice made Eva's heart break. 'And you could never take my place. I'm Father's right hand, whereas you...you're nothing but—' She stopped herself and, after a few seconds, stuck her nose in the air. 'Our guests are arriving shortly. Please don't be late to your own engagement party.'

Eva swallowed down her sorrow. 'I've no intention of being late. But neither do I have any intention of wearing a dress that has less material than thread holding it together.'

She strode to the giant George III armoire opposite the bed, even though her earlier inspection had shown less than a fraction of the items she'd left behind when she'd moved out on her twenty-first birthday.

These days she was content with her hostess's uniform when she was working or lounging in jeans and sweaters while she wrote her music on her days off. Haute couture, spa days and primping herself beautiful in order to please anyone were part of a past she'd happily left behind.

Unfortunately this time there'd been no escaping. Not when she alone had been able to find the solution to saving her family.

She tried in vain to squash the rising memories being back at Pennington Manor threatened to resurrect.

Zaccheo was in her past, a mistake that should never have happened. A reminder that ignoring a lesson learned only led to further heartache.

She sighed in relief when her hand closed on a silk wrap. The red dress would be far too revealing, a true spectacle for the three hundred guests her father had invited to gawp at. But at least the wrap would provide a little much-needed cover.

Glancing at the dress again, she shuddered.

She'd rather be anywhere but here, participating in this sham. But then hadn't her whole life been a sham? From parents who'd been publicly hailed as the couple to envy, but who'd fought bitterly in private until tragedy had struck in the form of her mother's cancer, to the lavish parties and expensive holidays that her father had secretly been borrowing money for, the Penningtons had been one giant sham for as long as Eva could remember.

Zaccheo's entry into their lives had only escalated her father's behaviour.

No, she refused to think about Zaccheo. He belonged to a chapter of her life that was firmly sealed. Tonight was about Harry Fairfield, her family's saviour, and her soon-to-be fiancé.

It was also about her father's health.

For that reason alone, she tried again with Sophie.

'For Father's sake, I want tonight to go smoothly, so can we try to get along?'

Sophie stiffened. 'If you're talking about Father's hospitalisation two weeks ago, I haven't forgotten.'

Watching her father struggle to breathe with what the doctors had termed a cardiac event had terrified Eva. It'd been the catalyst that had forced her to accept Harry's proposition.

'He's okay today, isn't he?' Despite her bitterness at her family's treatment of her, she couldn't help her concern for her remaining parent. Nor could she erase the secret yearning that the different version of the father she'd connected with very briefly after her mother's death, the one who wasn't an excess-loving megalomaniac who treated her as if she was an irritating inconvenience, hadn't been a figment of her imagination.

'He will be, once we get rid of the creditors threatening us with bankruptcy.'

Eva exhaled. There was no backing out; no secretly hoping that some other solution would present itself and save her from the sacrifice she was making.

All avenues had been thoroughly explored—Eva had demanded to see the Pennington books herself and spent a day with the company's accountants to verify that they were indeed in dire straits. Her father's rash acquisition of The Spire had stretched the company to breaking point. Harry Fairfield was their last hope.

She unzipped the red dress, resisting the urge to crush it into a wrinkled pulp.

'Do you need help?' Sophie asked, although Eva sensed the offer wasn't altruistic.

'No, I can manage.'

The same way she'd managed after her mother's death; through her father's rejection and Sophie's increasingly unreasonable behaviour; through the heartbreak of finding out about Zaccheo's betrayal.

Sophie nodded briskly. 'I'll see you downstairs, then.'

Eva slipped on the dress, avoiding another look in the mirror when the first glimpse showed what she'd feared most. Her every curve was accentuated, with large swathes of flesh exposed. With shaky fingers she applied her lipstick and slipped her feet into matching platform heels.

Slipping the gold and red wrap around her shoulders, she finally glanced at her image.

Chin up, girl. It's show time.

Eva wished the manageress of Siren were uttering the words, as she did every time before Eva stepped onto the stage.

Unfortunately, she wasn't at Siren. She'd promised to marry a man she didn't love, for the sake of saving her precious family name.

No amount of pep talk could stem the roaring agitation flooding her veins.

CHAPTER TWO

THE EVENT PLANNERS had outdone themselves. Potted palms, decorative screens and subdued lighting had been strategically placed around the main halls of Pennington Manor to hide the peeling plaster, chipped wood panelling and torn Aubusson rugs that funds could no longer stretch to rectify.

Eva sipped the champagne she'd been nursing for the last two hours and willed time to move faster. Technically she couldn't throw any guest out, but *Eight to Midnight* was the time the costly invitations had stated the party would last. She needed something to focus on or risk sliding into madness.

Gritting her teeth, she smiled as yet another guest demanded to see her engagement ring. The monstrous pink diamond's sole purpose was to demonstrate the Fairfields' wealth. Its alien weight dragged her hand down, hammering home the irrefutable point that she'd sold herself for her pedigree.

Her father's booming voice interrupted her maudlin thoughts. Surrounded by a group of influential politicians who hung onto his every word, Oscar Pennington was in his element.

Thickset but tall enough to hide the excess weight he carried, her father cut a commanding figure despite his recent spell in hospital. His stint in the army three decades ago had lent him a ruthless edge, cleverly counteracted by his natural charm. The combination made him enigmatic enough to attract attention when he walked into a room.

But not even that charisma had saved him from economic devastation four years ago.

With that coming close on the heels of her mother's illness, their social and economic circles had dwindled to nothing almost overnight, with her father desperately scrambling to hold things together.

End result—his association with Zaccheo Giordano.

Eva frowned, bewildered that her thoughts had circled back to the man she'd pushed to the dark recesses of her mind. A man she'd last seen being led away in handcuffs—

'There you are. I've been looking for you everywhere.'

Eva started, then berated herself for feeling guilty. Guilt belonged to those who'd committed crimes, who lied about their true motives.

Enough!

She smiled at Harry.

Her old university friend—a brilliant tech genius—had gone off the rails when he'd achieved fame and wealth straight out of university. Now a multimillionaire with enough money to bail out Penningtons, he represented her family's last hope.

'Well, you found me,' she said.

He was a few inches taller than her five feet four; she didn't have to look up too far to meet his twinkling soft brown eyes.

'Indeed. Are you okay?' he asked, his gaze reflecting concern.

'I'm fine,' she responded breezily.

He looked unconvinced. Harry was one of the few people who knew about her broken engagement to Zaccheo. He'd seen beneath her false smiles and assurances that she could handle a marriage of convenience and asked her point-blank if her past with Zaccheo Giordano would be a problem. Her swift *no* seemed to have satisfied him.

Now he looked unsure.

'Harry, don't fret. I can do this,' she insisted, despite the hollowness in her stomach.

He studied her solemnly, then called over a waiter and exchanged his empty champagne glass for a full one. 'If you say so, but I need advanced warning if this gets too weird for you, okay? My parents will have a fit if they read about me in the papers this side of Christmas.'

She nodded gratefully, then frowned. 'I thought you were going to take it easy tonight?' She indicated his glass.

'Gosh, you already sound like a wife.' He sniggered. 'Leave off, sweetness, the parents have already given me an earful.'

Having met his parents a week ago, Eva could imagine the exchange.

'Remember why *you're* doing this. Do you want to derail the PR campaign to clean up your image before it's even begun?'

While Harry couldn't care less about his social standing, his parents were voracious in their hunger for prestige and a pedigree to hang their name on. Only the threat to Harry's business dealings had finally forced him to address his reckless playboy image.

He took her arm and tilted his sand-coloured head affably towards hers. 'I promise to be on my best behaviour. Now that the tedious toasts have been made and we're officially engaged, it's time for the best part of the evening. The fireworks!'

Eva set her champagne glass down and stepped out of the dining-room alcove that had been her sanctuary throughout her childhood. 'Isn't that supposed to be a surprise?'

Harry winked. 'It is, but, since we've fooled everyone into thinking we're *madly* in love, faking our surprise should be easy.'

She smiled. 'I won't tell if you don't.'

Harry laid a hand across his heart. 'Thank you, my fair Lady Pennington.'

The reminder of why this whole sham engagement was happening slid like a knife between her ribs. Numbing herself to the pain, she walked out onto the terrace that overlooked the manor's multi-acre garden.

The gardens had once held large koi ponds, a giant summer house and an elaborate maze, but the prohibitive cost of the grounds' upkeep had led to the landscape being levelled and replaced with rolling carpet grass.

A smattering of applause greeted their arrival and Eva's gaze drifted over the guests to where Sophie, her father and Harry's parents stood watching them.

She caught her father's eye, and her stomach knotted.

While part of her was pleased that she'd found a solution to their family problems, she couldn't help but feel that nothing she did would ever bring her closer to her sister or father.

Her father might have accepted her help with the bail-out from Harry, but his displeasure at her chosen profession was yet another bone of contention between them. One she'd made clear she wouldn't back down on.

Turning away, she fixed her smile in place and exclaimed appropriately when the first elaborate firework display burst into the sky.

'So...my parents want us to live together,' Harry whispered in her ear.

'What?'

He laughed. 'Don't worry, I convinced them you hate my bachelor pad so we need to find a place that's *ours* rather than mine.'

Relief poured through her. 'Thank you.'

He brushed a hand down her cheek. 'You're welcome. But I deserve a reward for my sacrifice,' he said with a smile. 'How about dinner on Monday?'

'As long as it's not a paparazzi-stalked spectacle of a restaurant, you're on.'

'Great. It's a date.' He kissed her knuckles, much to the delight of the guests, who thought they were witnessing a true love match.

Eva allowed herself to relax. She might find what they were doing distasteful, but she was grateful that Harry's visit to Siren three weeks ago had ended up with him bailing her out, and not a calculating stranger.

'That dress is a knockout on you, by the way.'

She grimaced. 'It wasn't my first choice, but thank you.'

The next series of firework displays should've quieted the guests, yet murmurs around her grew.

'*Omigod*, whoever it is must have a death wish!' someone exclaimed.

Harry's eyes narrowed. 'I think we may have a last-minute guest.'

Eva looked around and saw puzzled gazes fixed at a point in the sky as the faint *thwopping* sound grew louder. Another set of fireworks went off, illuminating the looming object.

She frowned. 'Is that…?'

'A helicopter heading straight for the middle of the fireworks display? Yep. I guess the organisers decided to add another surprise to the party.'

'I don't think that's part of the entertainment,' Eva shouted to be heard over the descending aircraft.

Her heart slammed into her throat as a particularly elaborate firework erupted precariously close to the black-and-red chopper.

'Hell, if this is a stunt, I take my hat off to the pilot. It takes iron balls to fly into danger like that.' Harry chuckled.

The helicopter drew closer. Mesmerised, Eva watched it settle in the middle of the garden, her attention riveted to its single occupant.

The garden lights had been turned off to showcase the fireworks to maximum effect so she couldn't see who their unexpected guest was. Nevertheless, an ominous shiver chased up her spine.

She heard urgent shouts for the pyrotechnician to halt the display, but another rocket fizzed past the rotating blades.

A hush fell over the crowd as the helicopter door opened. A figure stepped out, clad from head to toe in black. As another blaze of colour filled the sky his body was thrown into relief.

Eva tensed as if she'd been shot with a stun gun.

It couldn't be...

He was behind bars, atoning for his ruthless greed. Eva squashed the sting of guilt that accompanied the thought.

Zaccheo Giordano and men of his ilk arrogantly believed they were above the law. They didn't deserve her sympathy, or the disloyal thought that he alone had paid the price when, by association, her father should've borne some of the blame. Justice ensured they went to jail and stayed there for the duration of their term. They weren't released early.

They certainly didn't land in the middle of a firework display at a private party as if they owned the land they walked on.

The spectacle unfolding before her stated differently.

Lights flickered on. Eva tracked the figure striding imperiously across the grass and up the wide steps.

Reaching the terrace, he paused and buttoned his single-breasted tuxedo.

'Oh, God,' she whispered.

'Wait...you know this bloke?' Harry asked, his tone for once serious.

Eva wanted to deny the man who now stood, easily head and shoulders above the nearest guests, his fierce, unwavering gaze pinned on her.

She didn't know whether to attribute the crackling electricity to his appearance or the look in his eyes. Both were viscerally menacing to the point of brutality.

The Zaccheo Giordano she'd had the misfortune of briefly tangling with before his incarceration had kept his hair trimmed short and his face clean-shaven.

This man had a full beard and his hair flowed over his shoulders in an unruly sea of thick jet waves. Eva swallowed at the pronounced difference in him. The sleek, almost gaunt man she'd known was gone. In his place breathed a Neanderthal with broader shoulders, thicker arms and a denser chest moulded by his black silk shirt. Equally dark trousers hugged lean hips and sturdy thighs to fall in a precise inch above expensive handmade shoes. But nothing of his attire disguised the aura he emanated.

Uncivilised. Explosively masculine. Lethal.

Danger vibrated from him like striations on baking asphalt. It flowed over the guests, who jostled each other for a better look at the impromptu visitor.

'Eva?' Harry's puzzled query echoed through her dazed consciousness.

Zaccheo released her from his deadly stare. His eyes flicked to the arm tucked into Harry's before he turned away. The breath exploded from her lungs. Sensing Harry about to ask another question, she nodded.

'Yes. That's Zaccheo.'

Her eyes followed Zaccheo as he turned towards her family.

Oscar's look of anger was laced with a heavy dose of apprehension. Sophie looked plain stunned.

Eva watched the man she'd hoped to never see again cup his hands behind his back and stroll towards her father. Anyone would've been foolish to think that stance indicated supplication. If anything, its severe mockery made Eva want to do the unthinkable and burst out laughing.

She would've, had she not been mired in deep dread at what Zaccheo's presence meant.

'Your ex?' Harry pressed.

She nodded numbly.

'Then we should say hello.'

Harry tugged on her arm and she realised too late what he meant.

'No. Wait!' she whispered fiercely.

But he was either too drunk or genuinely oblivious to the vortex of danger he was headed for to pay attention. The tension surrounding the group swallowed Eva as they approached. Heart pounding, she watched her father's and Zaccheo's gazes lock.

'I don't know what the hell you think you're doing here, Giordano, but I suggest you get back in that monstrosity and leave before I have you arrested for trespass.'

A shock wave went through the crowd.

Zaccheo didn't bat an eyelid.

'By all means do that if you wish, but you know exactly why I'm here, Pennington. We can play coy if you prefer. You'll be made painfully aware when I tire of it.' The words were barely above a murmur, but their venom raised the hairs on Eva's arms, triggering a gasp when she saw Sophie's face.

Her usually unflappable sister was severely agitated, her face distressingly pale.

'*Ciao*, Eva,' Zaccheo drawled without turning around. That deep, resonant voice, reminiscent of a tenor in a soulful opera, washed over her, its powerfully mesmerising quality reminding her how she'd once longed to hear him speak just for the hell of it. 'It's good of you to join us.'

'This is my engagement party. It's my duty to interact with my guests, even unwelcome ones who will be asked to leave immediately.'

'Don't worry, *cara*, I won't be staying long.'

The relief that surged up her spine disappeared when his gaze finally swung her way, then dropped to her left hand. With almost cavalier laziness, he caught her wrist and raised it to the light. He examined the ring for exactly three seconds. 'How predictable.'

He released her with the same carelessness he'd captured her.

Eva clenched her fist to stop the sizzling electricity firing up her arm at the brief contact.

'What's that supposed to mean?' Harry demanded.

Zaccheo levelled steely grey eyes on him, then his parents. 'This is a private discussion. Leave us.'

Peter Fairfield's laugh held incredulity, the last inch of

champagne in his glass sloshing wildly as he raised his arm. 'I think you've got the wrong end of the stick there, mate. You're the one who needs to take a walk.'

Eva caught Harry's pained look at his father's response, but could do nothing but watch, heart in her throat, as Zaccheo faced Peter Fairfield.

Again she was struck by how much his body had changed; how the sleek, layered muscle lent a deeper sense of danger. Whereas before it'd been like walking close to the edge of a cliff, looking into his eyes now was like staring into a deep, bottomless abyss.

'Would you care to repeat that, *il mio amico*?' The almost conversational tone belied the savage tension beneath the words.

'Oscar, who *is* this?' Peter Fairfield demanded of her father, who seemed to have lost the ability to speak after Zaccheo's succinct taunt.

Eva inserted herself between the two men before the situation got out of hand. Behind her, heat from Zaccheo's body burned every exposed inch of skin. Ignoring the sensation, she cleared her throat.

'Mr and Mrs Fairfield, Harry, we'll only be a few minutes. We're just catching up with Mr Giordano.' She glanced at her father. A vein throbbed in his temple and he'd gone a worrying shade of puce. Fear climbed into her heart. 'Father?'

He roused himself and glanced around. A charming smile slid into place, but it was off by a light year. The trickle of ice that had drifted down her spine at Zaccheo's unexpected arrival turned into a steady drip.

'We'll take this in my study. Don't hesitate to let the staff know if you need anything.' He strode away, followed by a disturbingly quiet Sophie.

Zaccheo's gaze swung to Harry, who defiantly withstood the laser gaze for a few seconds before he glanced at her.

'Are you sure?' Harry asked, that touching concern again in his eyes.

Her instinct screamed a terrible foreboding, but she nodded. 'Yes.'

'Okay. Hurry back, sweetness.' Before she could move, he dropped a kiss on her mouth.

A barely audible lethal growl charged through the air.

Eva flinched.

She wanted to face Zaccheo. Demand that he crawl back behind the bars that should've been holding him. But that glimpse of fear in her father's eyes stopped her. She tugged the wrap closer around her.

Something wasn't right here. She was willing to bet the dilapidated ancestral pile beneath her feet that something was seriously, *dangerously* wrong—

'Move, Eva.'

The cool command spoken against her ear sent shivers coursing through her.

She moved, only because the quicker she got to the bottom of why he was here, the quicker he would leave. But with each step his dark gaze probed her back, making the walk to her father's study on the other side of the manor the longest in her life.

Zaccheo shut the door behind him. Her father turned from where he'd been gazing into the unlit fireplace. Again Eva spotted apprehension in his eyes before he masked it.

'Whatever grievance you think you have the right to air, I suggest you rethink it, son. Even if this were the right time or place—'

'I am *not* your son, Pennington.' Zaccheo's response held lethal bite, the first sign of his fury breaking through. 'As for why I'm here, I have five thousand three hundred and twenty-two pieces of documentation that proves you colluded with various other individuals to pin a crime on me that I didn't commit.'

'What?' Eva gasped, then the absurdity of the statement made her shake her head. 'We don't believe you.'

Zaccheo's eyes remained on her father. 'You may not, but your father does.'

Oscar Pennington laughed, but the sound lacked its usual boom and zest. When sweat broke out over his forehead, fear gripped Eva's insides.

She steeled her spine. 'Our lawyers will rip whatever evidence you think you have to shreds, I'm sure. If you're here to seek some sort of closure, you picked the wrong time to do it. Perhaps we can arrange to meet you at some other time?'

Zaccheo didn't move. Didn't blink. Hands once again tucked behind his back, he simply watched her father, his body a coiled predator waiting to strike a fatal blow.

Silence stretched, throbbed with unbearable menace. Eva looked from her father to Sophie and back again, her dread escalating. 'What's going on?' she demanded.

Her father gripped the mantel until his knuckles shone white. 'You chose the wrong enemy. You're sorely mistaken if you think I'll let you blackmail me in my own home.'

Sophie stepped forward. 'Father, don't—'

'Good, you haven't lost your hubris.' Zaccheo's voice slashed across her sister's. 'I was counting on that. Here's what I'm going to do. In ten minutes I'm going to leave here with Eva, right in front of all your guests. You won't lift a finger to stop me. You'll tell them exactly who I am. Then you'll make a formal announcement that I'm the man your daughter will marry two weeks from today and that I have your blessing. I don't want to trust something so important to phone cameras and social media, although your guests will probably do a pretty good job. I noticed a few members of the press out there, so that part of your task should be easy. If the articles are written to my satisfaction, I'll be in touch on Monday to lay out how you can begin to make reparations to me. However, if by the time Eva and I wake up tomorrow morning the news of our engagement isn't in the press, then all bets are off.'

Oscar Pennington's breathing altered alarmingly. His

mouth opened but no words emerged. In the arctic silence that greeted Zaccheo's deadly words, Eva gaped at him.

'You're clearly not in touch with all of your faculties if you think those ridiculous demands are going to be met.' When silence greeted her response, she turned sharply to her father. 'Father? Why aren't you saying something?' she demanded, although the trepidation beating in her chest spelled its own doom.

'Because he can't, Eva. Because he's about to do exactly as I say.'

She rounded on him, and was once again rocked to the core by Zaccheo's visually powerful, utterly captivating transformation. So much so, she couldn't speak for several seconds. 'You're out of your mind!' she finally blurted.

Zaccheo's gaze didn't stray from its laser focus on her father. 'Believe me, *cara mia*, I haven't been saner than I am in this moment.'

CHAPTER THREE

ZACCHEO WATCHED EVA'S head swivel to her father, confusion warring with anger.

'Go on, Oscar. She's waiting for you to tell me to go to hell. Why don't you?'

Pennington staggered towards his desk, his face ashen and his breathing growing increasingly laboured.

'Father!' Eva rushed to his side—ignoring the poisonous look her sister sent her—as he collapsed into his leather armchair.

Zaccheo wanted to rip her away, let her watch her father suffer as his sins came home to roost. Instead he allowed the drama to play out. The outcome would be inevitable and would only go one way.

His way.

He wanted to look into Pennington's eyes and see the defeat and helplessness the other man had expected to see in his eyes the day Zaccheo had been sentenced.

Both sisters now fussed over their father and a swell of satisfaction rose at the fear in their eyes. Eva glanced his way and he experienced a different punch altogether. One he'd thought himself immune to, but had realised otherwise the moment he'd stepped off his helicopter and singled her out in the crowd.

That unsettling feeling, as if he were suffering from vertigo despite standing on terra firma, had intrigued and annoyed him in equal measures from the very first time he'd seen her, her voice silkily hypnotic as she crooned into a mic on a golden-lit stage, her fingers caressing the black microphone stand as if she were touching a lover.

Even knowing exactly who she was, what she represented,

he hadn't been able to walk away. In the weeks after their first meeting, he'd fooled himself into believing she was different, that she wasn't tainted with the same greed to further her pedigree by whatever means necessary; that she wasn't willing to do whatever it took to secure her family's standing, even while secretly scorning his upbringing.

Her very public denouncement of any association between them on the day of his sentencing had been the final blow. Not that Zaccheo hadn't had the scales viciously ripped from his eyes by then.

No, by that fateful day fourteen months ago, he'd known just how thoroughly he'd been suckered.

'What the hell do you think you're doing?' she muttered fiercely, her moss-green eyes firing lasers at him.

Zaccheo forced himself not to smile. The time for gloating would come later. 'Exacting the wages of sin, *dolcezza*. What else?'

'I don't know what you're talking about, but I don't think my father is in a position to have a discussion with you right now, Mr Giordano.'

Her prim and proper tones bit savagely into Zaccheo, wiping away any trace of twisted mirth. That tone said he ought to *know his place*, that he ought to stand there like a good little servant and wait to be addressed instead of upsetting the lord of the manor with his petty concerns.

Rage bubbled beneath his skin, threatening to erupt. Blunt nails bit into his wrist, but the pain wasn't enough to calm his fury. He clenched his jaw for a long moment before he trusted himself to speak.

'I gave you ten minutes, Pennington. You now have five. I suggest you practise whatever sly words you'll be using to address your guests.' Zaccheo shrugged. 'Or not. Either way, things *will* go my way.'

Eva rushed at him, her striking face and flawless skin flushed with a burst of angry colour as she stopped a few feet away.

Out on the terrace, he'd compelled himself not to stare too long at her in case he betrayed his feelings. In case his gaze devoured her as he'd wanted to do since her presence snaked like a live wire inside him.

Now, he took in that wild gypsy-like caramel-blonde hair so out of place in this polished stratosphere her family chose to inhabit. The striking contrast between her bright hair, black eyebrows and dark-rimmed eyes had always fascinated him. But no more than her cupid-bow lips, soft, dark red and sinfully sensual. Or the rest of her body.

'You assume I have no say in whatever despicable spectacle you're planning. That I intend to meekly stand by while you humiliate my family? Well, think again!'

'Eva...' her father started.

'No! I don't know what exactly is going on here, but I intend to play no part in it.'

'You'll play your part, and you'll play it well,' Zaccheo interjected, finally driving his gaze up from the mouth he wanted to feast on more than he wanted his next breath. *That'll come soon enough*, he promised himself.

'Or what? You'll carry through with your empty threats?'

His fury eased a touch and twisted amusement slid back into place. It never ceased to amaze him how the titled rich felt they were above the tenets that governed ordinary human beings. His own stepfather had been the same. He'd believed, foolishly, that his pedigree and connections would insulate him from his reckless business practices, that the Old Boys' Club would provide a safety net despite his poor judgement.

Zaccheo had taken great pleasure in watching his mother's husband squirm before him, cap in hand, when Zaccheo had bought his family business right from underneath his pompous nose. But even then, the older man had continued to treat him like a third-class citizen...

Just as Oscar Pennington had done. Just as Eva Pennington was doing now.

'You think my threats empty?' he enquired softly. 'Then do nothing. It's after all your privilege and your right.'

Something of the lethal edge that rode him must have transmitted itself to her. Apprehension chased across her face before she firmed those impossibly sumptuous lips.

'Do nothing, and watch me bury your family in the deepest, darkest, most demeaning pit you can dream of. Do nothing and watch me unleash a scandal the scale of which you can only imagine on your precious family name.' He bared his teeth in a mirthless smile and her eyes widened in stunned disbelief. 'It would be *my* privilege and pleasure to do so.'

Oscar Pennington inhaled sharply and Zaccheo's gaze zeroed in on his enemy. The older man rose from the chair. Though he looked frail, his eyes reflected icy disdain. But Zaccheo also glimpsed the fear of a cornered man weighing all the options to see how to escape the noose dangling ever closer.

Zaccheo smiled inwardly. He had no intention of letting Pennington escape. Not now, not ever.

The flames of retribution intensifying within him, he unclasped his hands. It was time to bring this meeting to an end.

'Your time's up, Pennington.'

Eva answered instead of her father. 'How do we know you're not bluffing? You say you have something over us, prove it,' she said defiantly.

He could've walked out and let them twist in the wind of uncertainty. Pennington would find out soon enough the length of Zaccheo's ruthless reach. But the thought of leaving Eva here when he departed was suddenly unthinkable. So far he'd allowed himself a brief glimpse of her body wrapped in that obscenely revealing red dress. But that one glimpse had been enough. Quite apart from the rage boiling his blood, the steady hammer of his pulse proved that he still wanted her with a fever that spiked higher with each passing second.

He would take what he'd foolishly and piously denied

himself two years ago. He would *take* and *use*, just as they'd done to him. Only when he'd achieved every goal he'd set himself would he feel avenged.

'You can't, can you?' Oscar taunted with a sly smile, bringing Zaccheo back to the room and the three aristocratic faces staring at him with varying degrees of disdain and fear.

He smiled, almost amused by the older man's growing confidence. 'Harry Fairfield is providing you with a bridging loan of fifteen million pounds because the combined running costs of the Pennington Hotels and The Spire have you stretched so thin the banks won't touch you. While you desperately drum up an adequate advertising budget to rent out all those overpriced but empty floors in The Spire, the interest owed to the Chinese consortium who own seventy-five per cent of the building is escalating. You have a meeting with them on Monday to request more time to pay the interest. In return for Fairfield's investment, you're handing him your daughter.'

Eva glared at him. 'So you've asked a few questions about Penningtons' business practices. That doesn't empower you to make demands of any of us.'

Zaccheo took a moment to admire her newfound grit. During their initial association, she'd been a little more timid, and in her father's shadow, but it looked as if the kitten had grown a few claws. He curbed the thrill at what was to come and answered.

'Yes, it does. Would you be interested to know the Chinese consortium sold their seventy-five per cent of The Spire to me three days ago? So by my calculation you're in excess of three months late on interest payments, correct?'

A rough sound, a cross between a cough and a wheeze, escaped Pennington's throat. There was no class or grace in the way he gaped at Zaccheo. He dropped back into his chair, his face a mask of hatred.

'I knew you were a worthless bet the moment I set eyes on you. I should've listened to my instincts.'

The red haze he'd been trying to hold back surged higher. 'No, what you wanted was a spineless scapegoat, a *capro espiatorio*, who would make you rich and fat and content and even give up his life without question!'

'Mr Giordano, surely we can discuss this like sensible business-minded individuals,' Sophie Pennington advanced, her hands outstretched in benign sensibility. Zaccheo looked from the hands she willed not to tremble to the veiled disdain in her eyes. Then he looked past her to Eva, who'd returned to her father's side, her face pale but her eyes shooting her displeasure at him.

Unexpectedly and very much unwelcome, a tiny hint of compassion tugged at him.

Basta!

He turned abruptly and reached for the door handle. 'You have until I ready my chopper for take-off to come to me, Eva.' He didn't need to expand on that edict. The *or else* hung in the air like the deadly poison he intended it to be.

He walked out and headed for the terrace, despite every nerve in his body straining to return to the room and forcibly drag Eva out.

True, he hadn't bargained for the visceral reaction to seeing her again. And yes, he hadn't quite been able to control his reaction to seeing another man's ring on her finger, that vulgar symbol of ownership hollowing out his stomach. The knowledge that she'd most likely shared that hapless drunk's bed, given the body he'd once believed to be his to another, ate through his blood like acid on metal. But he couldn't afford to let his emotions show.

Every strategic move in this game of deadly retribution hinged on him maintaining his control; on not letting them see how affected he was by all this.

He stepped onto the terrace and all conversation ceased. Curious faces gaped and one or two bolder guests even tried to intercept him. Zaccheo cut through the crowd, his gaze on the chopper a few dozen yards away.

She would come to him. As an outcome of his first salvo, nothing else would be acceptable.

His pulse thudded loud and insistent in his ears as he strolled down the steps towards the aircraft. The fireworks amid which he'd landed had long since gone quiet, but the scent of sulphur lingered in the air, reminding him of the volatility that lingered beneath his own skin, ready to erupt at the smallest trigger.

He wouldn't let it erupt. Not yet.

A murmur rose behind him, the fevered excitement that came with the anticipation of a spectacle. A *scandal*.

Zaccheo compelled himself to keep walking.

He ducked beneath the powerful rotors of his aircraft and reached for the door.

'Wait!'

He stopped. Turned.

Three hundred pairs of eyes watched with unabashed interest as Eva paused several feet from him.

Behind her, her father and sister stood on the steps, wearing similar expressions of dread. Zaccheo wanted them to stew for a while longer, but he found his attention drawn to the woman striding towards him. Her face reflected more defiance than dread. It also held pride and not a small measure of bruised disdain. Zaccheo vowed in that moment to make her regret that latter look, make her take back every single moment she'd thought herself above him.

Swallowing, he looked down at her body.

She held the flimsy wrap around her like armour. As if that would protect her from him. With one ruthless tug, he pulled it away. It fluttered to the ground, revealing her luscious, heart-stopping figure to his gaze. Unable to stem the frantic need crashing through him, he stepped forward and speared his fingers into the wild tumble of her hair.

Another step and she was in his arms.

Where she belonged.

* * *

The small pocket of air Eva had been able to retain in her lungs during her desperate flight after Zaccheo evaporated when he yanked her against him. Her body went from shivering in the crisp January air to furnace-hot within seconds. The fingers in her hair tightened, his other arm sliding around her waist.

Eva wanted to remain unaffected, slam her hands against his chest and remove herself from that dangerous wall of masculinity. But she couldn't move. So she fought with her words.

'You may think you've won, that you own me, but you don't,' she snapped. 'You never will!'

His eyes gleamed. 'Such fire. Such determination. You've changed, *cara mia*, I'll give you that. And yet here you are, barely one minute after I walked out of your father's study. Mere hours after you promised yourself to another man, here you are, Eva Pennington, ready to promise yourself to me. Ready to become whatever I want you to be.'

Her snigger made his eyes narrow, but she didn't care. 'Keep telling yourself that. I look forward to your shock when I prove you wrong.'

That deadly smile she'd first seen in her father's study reappeared, curling fear through her. It reeked with far too much gratification to kill that unshakeable sensation that she was standing on the edge of a precipice, and that, should she fall, there would be no saving her.

She realised the reason for the smile when he lifted her now bare fingers to his eye level. 'You've proved me right already.'

'Are you completely sure about that?' The question was a bold but empty taunt.

The lack of fuss with which Harry had taken back his ring a few minutes ago had been a relief.

She might not have an immediate solution to her family's

problems, but Eva was glad she no longer had to pretend she was half of a sham couple.

Zaccheo brought her fingers to his mouth and kissed her ring finger, stunning her back to reality. Flashes erupted as his actions were recorded, no doubt to be streamed across the fastest mediums available.

Recalling the conversation she'd just had with her father, she tried to pull away. 'This pound-of-flesh taking isn't going to last very long, so I suggest you enjoy it while it lasts. I intend to return to my life before midnight—'

Her words dried up when his face closed in a mask of icy fury, and his hands sealed her body even closer to his.

'Your first lesson is to stop speaking to me as if I'm the hired help. Refraining from doing so will put me in a much calmer frame of mind to deal with you than otherwise,' he said with unmistakeable warning.

Eva doubted that anyone had dared to speak to Zaccheo Giordano in the way he referred, but she wasn't about to debate that point with him with three hundred pairs of eyes watching. She was struggling enough to keep upright what with all the turbulent sensations firing through her at his touch. 'Why, Zaccheo, you sound as if you've a great many lessons you intend to dole out...' She tried to sound bored, but her voice emerged a little too breathless for her liking.

'Patience, *cara mia*. You'll be instructed as and when necessary.' His gaze dropped to her mouth and her breath lodged in her sternum. 'For now, I wish the talking to cease.'

He closed the final inch between them and slanted his mouth over hers. The world tilted and shook beneath her feet. Expertly sensual and demanding, he kissed her as if he owned her mouth, as if he owned her whole body. In all her adult years, Eva had never imagined the brush of a beard would infuse her with such spine-tingling sensations. Yet she shivered with fiery delight as Zaccheo's silky facial hair caressed the corners of her mouth.

She groaned at the forceful breach of his tongue. Her arms drifted over his taut biceps as she became lost in the potent magic of his kiss. At the first touch of his tongue against hers, she shuddered. He made a rough sound and his sharp inhalation vibrated against her. His fingers convulsed in her hair and his other hand drifted to her bottom, moulding her as he stepped back against the aircraft and widened his stance to bring her closer.

Eva wasn't sure how long she stood there, adrift in a swirl of sensation as he ravaged her mouth. It wasn't until her lungs screamed and her heart jackhammered against her ribs did she recall where she was…what was happening.

And still she wanted to continue.

So much so she almost moaned in protest when firm hands set her back and she found herself staring into molten eyes dark with savage hunger.

'I think we've given our audience enough to feed on. Get in.'

The calm words, spoken in direct counteraction to the frenzied look in his eyes, doused Eva with cold reality. That she'd made even more of a spectacle of herself hit home as wolf whistles ripped through the air.

'This was all for *show*?' she whispered numbly, shivering in the frigid air.

One sleek eyebrow lifted. 'Of course. Did you think I wanted to kiss you because I was so desperate for you I just couldn't help myself? You'll find that I have more self-restraint than that. Get in,' he repeated, holding the steel and glass door to the aircraft open.

Eva brushed cold hands over her arms, unable to move. She stared at him, perhaps hoping to find some humanity in the suddenly grim-faced block of stone in front of her. Or did she want a hint of the man who'd once framed her face in his hands and called her the most beautiful thing in his life?

Of course, that had been a lie. Everything about Zaccheo

had been a lie. Still she probed for some softness beneath that formidable exterior.

His implacable stare told her she was grasping at straws, as she had from the very beginning, when she'd woven stupid dreams around him.

A gust of icy wind blew across the grass, straight into her exposed back. A flash of red caught her eye and she blindly stumbled towards the terrace. She'd barely taken two steps when he seized her arm.

'What the hell do you think you're doing?' Zaccheo enquired frostily.

'I'm cold,' she replied through chattering teeth. 'My wrap...' She pointed to where the material had drifted.

'Leave it. This will keep you warm.' With one smooth move, he unbuttoned, shrugged off his tuxedo and draped it around her shoulders. The sudden infusion of warmth was overwhelming. Eva didn't want to drown in the distinctively heady scent of the man who was wrecking her world, didn't welcome her body's traitorous urge to burrow into the warm silk lining. And most of all, she didn't want to be beholden to him in any way, or accept any hint of kindness from him.

Zaccheo Giordano had demonstrated a ruthless thirst to annihilate those he deemed enemies in her father's study.

But she was no longer the naive and trusting girl she'd been a year and a half ago. Zaccheo's betrayal and her continued fraught relationship with her father and sister had hardened her heart. The pain was still there—would probably always be there—but so were the new fortifications against further hurt. She had no intention of laying her heart and soul bare to further damage from the people she'd once blithely believed would return the same love and devotion she offered freely.

She started to shrug off the jacket. 'No, thanks. I'd prefer not to be stamped as your possession.'

He stopped her by placing both hands on her arms.

Dark grey eyes pinned her to the spot, the sharper, icier

burst of wind whipping around them casting him in a dead-
lier, more dangerous light.

'You're already my possession. You became mine the moment you made the choice to follow me out here, Eva. You
can kid yourself all you want, but this is your reality from
here on in.'

CHAPTER FOUR

@Ladystclare OMG! Bragging rights=mine! Beheld fireworks w/in fireworks @P/Manor last night when LadyP eloped w/convict lover! #amazeballs

@Aristokitten Bet it was all a publicity stunt, but boy that kiss? Sign me up! #Ineedlatinlovelikethat

@Countrypile That wasn't love. That was an obscene and shameless money-grabbing gambit at its worst! #Donotencouragerancidbehaviour

EVA FLINCHED, her stomach churning at each new message that flooded her social-media stream.

The hours had passed in a haze after Zaccheo flew them from Pennington Manor. In solid command of the helicopter, he'd soared over the City of London and landed on the vertiginous rooftop of The Spire.

The stunning split-level penthouse's interior had barely registered in the early hours when Zaccheo's enigmatic aide, Romeo, had directed the butler to show her to her room.

Zaccheo had stalked away without a word, leaving her in the middle of his marble-tiled hallway, clutching his jacket.

Sleep had been non-existent in the bleak hours that had followed. At five a.m., she'd given up and taken a quick shower before putting on that skin-baring dress again.

Wishing she'd asked for a blanket to cover the acres of flesh on display, she cringed as another salacious offering popped into her inbox displayed on Zaccheo's tablet.

Like a spectator frozen on the fringes of an unfolding train wreck, she read the latest post.

@Uberwoman Hey ConvictLover, that flighty poor little rich girl is wasted on you. Real women exist. Let ME rock your world!

Eva curled her fist, refusing to entertain the image of any woman rocking Zaccheo's world. She didn't care one way or the other. If she had a choice, she would be ten thousand miles away from this place.

'If you're thinking of responding to any of that, consider yourself warned against doing so.'

She jumped at the deep voice a whisper from her ear. She'd thought she would be alone in the living room for at least another couple of hours before dealing with Zaccheo. Now she wished she'd stayed in her room.

She stood and faced him, the long black suede sofa between them no barrier to Zaccheo's towering presence.

'I've no intention of responding. And you really shouldn't sneak up on people like that,' she tagged on when the leisurely drift of those incisive eyes over her body made her feel like a specimen under a microscope.

'I don't sneak. Had you been less self-absorbed in your notoriety, you would've heard me enter the room.'

Anger welled up. 'You accuse *me* of being notorious? All this is happening because *you* insisted on gatecrashing a private event and turning it into a public spectacle.'

'And, of course, you were so eager to find out whether you're trending that you woke up at dawn to follow the news.'

She wanted to ask how he'd known what time she'd left her room, but Eva suspected she wouldn't like the answer. 'You assume I slept at all when sleep was the last thing on my mind, having been blackmailed into coming here. And, FYI, I don't read the gutter press. Not unless I want the worst kind of indigestion.'

He rounded the sofa and stopped within arm's length. She stood her ground, but she couldn't help herself ogling the breathtaking body filling her vision.

It was barely six o'clock and yet he looked as vitally masculine as if he'd been up and ready for hours. A film of sweat covered the hair-dusted arms beneath the pulled-up sleeves, and his damp white T-shirt moulded his chiselled torso. His black drawstring sweatpants did nothing to hide thick thighs and Eva struggled to avert her gaze from the virile outline of his manhood against the soft material. Dragging her gaze up, she stared in fascination at the hands and fingers wrapped in stained boxing gauze.

'Do you intend to spend the rest of the morning ogling me, Eva?' he asked mockingly.

She looked into his eyes and that potent, electric tug yanked hard at her. Reminding herself that she was immune from whatever spell he'd once cast on her, she raised her chin.

'I intend to attempt a reasonable conversation with you in the cold light of day regarding last night's events.'

'That suggests you believe our previous interactions have been unreasonable?'

'I did a quick search online. You were released yesterday morning. It stands to reason that you're still a little affected by your incarceration—'

His harsh, embittered laugh bounced like bullets around the room. Eva folded her arms, refusing to cower at the sound.

He stepped towards her, the tension in his body barely leashed. 'You think I'm a *"little affected"* by my incarceration? Tell me, *bella*,' he invited softly, 'do you know what it feels like to be locked in a six-by-ten, damp and rancid cage for over a year?'

A brief wave of torment overcame his features, and a different tug, one of sympathy, pulled at her. Then she reminded herself just who she was dealing with. 'Of course not. I just don't want you to do anything that you'll regret.'

'Your touching concern for my welfare is duly noted. But I suggest you save it for yourself. Last night was merely you and your family being herded into the eye of the storm. The real devastation is just getting started.'

As nightmarish promises went, Zaccheo's chilled her to the bone. Before she could reply, several pings blared from the tablet. She glanced down and saw more lurid posts about what *real women* wanted to do to Zaccheo.

She shut the tablet and straightened to find him slowly unwinding the gauze from his right hand, his gaze pinned on her. Silence stretched as he freed both hands and tossed the balled cloth onto the glass-topped coffee table.

'So, do I get any sort of itinerary for this impending apocalypse?' she asked when it became clear he was content to let the silence linger.

One corner of his mouth lifted. 'We'll have breakfast in half an hour. After that, we'll see whether your father has done what I demanded of him. If he has, we'll take it from there.'

Recalling her father's overly belligerent denial once Zaccheo had left the study last night, anxiety skewered her. 'And if he hasn't?'

'Then his annihilation will come sooner rather than later.'

Half an hour later, Eva struggled to swallow a mouthful of buttered toast and quickly chased it down with a sip of tea before she choked.

A few minutes ago, a brooding Romeo had entered with the butler who'd delivered a stack of broadsheets. The other man had conversed in Italian with a freshly showered and even more visually devastating Zaccheo.

Zaccheo's smile after the short exchange had incited her first panic-induced emotion. He'd said nothing after Romeo left. Instead he'd devoured a hearty plate of scrambled eggs, grilled mushrooms and smoked pancetta served on Italian bread with unsettling gusto.

But as the silence spread thick and cloying across the room she finally set her cup down and glanced to where he stood now at the end of the cherrywood dining table, his hands braced on his hips, an inscrutable expression on his face.

Again, Eva was struck by the change in him. Even now he was dressed more formally in dark grey trousers and a navy shirt with the sleeves rolled up, her eyes were drawn to the gladiator-like ruggedness of his physique.

'Eva.' Her name was a deep command. One she desperately wanted to ignore. It held a quiet triumph she didn't want to acknowledge. The implications were more than she could stomach. She wasn't one for burying her head in the sand, but if her father had done what Zaccheo had demanded, then—

'Eva,' he repeated. Sharper. Controlled but demanding.

Heart hammering, she glanced at him. 'What?'

He stared back without blinking, his body deathly still. 'Come here.'

Refusing to show how rattled she was, she stood, teetered on the heels she'd had no choice but to wear again, and strode towards him.

He tracked her with chilling precision, his eyes dropping to her hips for a charged second before he looked back up. Eva hated her body for reacting to that look, even as her breasts tingled and a blaze lit between her thighs.

Silently she cursed herself. She had no business reacting to that look, or to any man on any plane of emotion whatsoever. She had proof that path only ended in eviscerating heartache.

She stopped a few feet from him, made sure to place a dining chair between them. But the solid wood couldn't stop her senses from reacting to his scent, or her nipples from furling into tight, needy buds when her gaze fell on the golden gleam of his throat revealed by the gap in his shirt. Quickly crossing her arms, she looked down at the newspapers.

That they'd made headlines was unmistakeable. Bold black letters and exclamation marks proclaimed Zaccheo's antics. And as for *that* picture of them locked together...

'I can't believe you landed a helicopter in the middle of a fireworks display,' she threw out, simply because it was easier than acknowledging the other words written on the page binding her to Zaccheo, insinuating they were something they would never be.

He looked from her face to the front-page picture showing him landing his helicopter during a particularly violent explosion. 'Were you concerned for me?' he mocked.

'Of course not. You obviously don't care about your own safety so why should I?'

A simmering silence followed, then he stalked closer. 'I hope you intend to act a little more concerned towards my well-being once we're married.'

Any intention of avoiding looking at him fled her mind. '*Married?* Don't you think you've taken this far enough?' she snapped.

'Excuse me?'

'You wanted to humiliate my father. Congratulations, you've made headlines in every single newspaper. Don't you think it's time to drop this?'

His eyes turned into pools of ice. 'You think this is some sort of game?' he enquired silkily.

'What else can it be? If you really had the evidence you claim to have, why haven't you handed it over to the police?'

'You believe I'm bluffing?' His voice was a sharp blade slicing through the air.

'I believe you feel aggrieved.'

'Really? And what else did you *believe*?'

Eva refused to quail beneath the look that threatened to cut her into pieces. 'It's clear you want to make some sort of statement about how you were treated by my father. You've done that now. Let it go.'

'So your father did all this—' he indicated the papers '—just to stop me throwing a childish tantrum? And what about you? Did you throw yourself at my feet to buy your family time to see how long my bluff would last?'

She flung her arms out in exasperation. 'Come on, Zaccheo—'

They both stilled at her use of his name. Eva had no time to recover from the unwitting slip. Merciless fingers speared into her hair, much as they had last night, holding her captive as his thumb tilted her chin.

'How far are you willing to go to get me to be *reasonable*? Or perhaps I should guess? After all, just last night you'd dropped to an all-time low of whoring yourself to a drunken boy in order to save your family.' The thick condemnation feathered across her skin.

Rage flared in her belly, gave her the strength to remain upright. He stood close. Far too close. She stepped back, but only managed to wedge herself between the table and Zaccheo's towering body. 'As opposed to what? Whoring myself to a middle-aged criminal?'

He leaned down, crowding her further against the polished wood. 'You know exactly how old I am. In fact, I recall precisely where we both were when the clock struck midnight on my thirtieth birthday. Or perhaps you need me to refresh your memory?' His smooth, faintly accented voice trailed amused contempt.

'Don't bother—'

'I'll do it anyway, it's no hardship,' he offered, as if her sharp denial hadn't been uttered. 'We were newly engaged, and you were on your knees in front of my penthouse window, uncaring that anyone with a pair of decent binoculars would see us. All you cared about was getting your busy, greedy little hands on my belt, eager to rid me of my trousers so you could wish me a happy birthday in a way most men fantasise about.'

Her skin flushed with a wave of heat so strong, she feared spontaneous combustion. 'That wasn't my idea.'

One brow quirked. 'Was it not?'

'No, you dared me to do it.'

His mouth twitched. 'Are you saying I forced you?'

Those clever fingers were drifting along her scalp, lazily caressing, lulling her into showing her vulnerability.

Eva sucked in a deep breath. 'I'm saying I don't want to talk about the past. I prefer to stick to the present.'

She didn't want to remember how gullible she'd been back then, how stupidly eager to please, how excited she'd been that this god of a man, who could have any woman he wanted with a lazy crook of his finger, had pursued *her*, chosen *her*.

Even after learning the hard way that men in positions of power would do anything to stay in that power, that her two previous relationships had only been a means to an end for the men involved, she'd still allowed herself to believe Zaccheo wanted her for herself. Finding out that he was no better, that he only wanted her to secure a *business deal*, had delivered a blow she'd spent the better part of a year burying in a deep hole.

At first his demands had been subtle: a business dinner here, a charity event there—occasions she'd been proud and honoured to accompany him on. Until that fateful night when she'd overheard a handful of words that had had the power to sting like nothing else.

She's the means to an end. Nothing more...

The conversation that had followed remained seared into her brain. Zaccheo, impatiently shutting her down, then brazenly admitting he'd said those words. That he'd used her.

Most especially, she recalled the savage pain in knowing she had got him so wrong, had almost given herself to a man who held such careless regard for her, and only cared about her pedigree.

And yet his shock when she'd returned his ring had made her wonder whether she'd done the right thing.

His arrest days later for criminal negligence had confirmed what sort of man she'd foolishly woven her dreams around.

She met his gaze now. 'You got what you wanted—your name next to mine on the front page. The whole world knows I left with you last night, that I'm no longer engaged to Harry.'

His hand slipped to her nape, worked over tense muscles. 'And how did Fairfield take being so unceremoniously dumped?' he asked.

'Harry cares about me, so he was a complete gentleman about it. Shame I can't say the same about you.'

Dark grey eyes gleamed dangerously. 'You mean he wasn't torn up at the thought of never having access to this body again?' he mocked.

She lifted a brow. 'Never say never.'

Tension coiled his body. 'If you think I'll tolerate any further interaction between you and Fairfield, you're severely mistaken,' he warned with a dark rumble.

'Why, Zaccheo, you sound almost jealous.'

Heat scoured his cheekbones and a tiny part of her quailed at her daring. 'You'd be wise to stop testing me, *dolcezza*.'

'If you want this to stop, tell me why you're doing this.'

'I'm only going to say it one more time, so let it sink in. I don't intend to stop until your father's reputation is in the gutter and everything he took from me is returned, plus interest.'

'Can I see the proof of what you accuse my father of?'

'Would you believe even if you saw it? Or will you cling to the belief that I'm the big, bad ogre who's just throwing his weight about?' he taunted.

Eva looked down at the papers on the table, every last one containing everything Zaccheo had demanded. Would her father have done it if Zaccheo's threats were empty?

'Last night, when you said you and I…' She stopped, unable to process the reality.

'Would be married in two weeks? *Sì*, I meant that, too. And to get that ball rolling, we're going shopping for an engagement ring in exactly ten minutes, after which we have a full day ahead, so if you require further sustenance I suggest you finish your breakfast.'

He dropped his fingers from her nape and stepped back. With a last look filled with steely determination, he picked up the closest paper and walked out of the room.

CHAPTER FIVE

THEIR FIRST STOP was an exclusive coat boutique in Bond Street. Zaccheo told himself it was because he didn't want to waste time. The truth mocked him in the form of needing to cover Eva Pennington's body before he lost any more brain cells to the lust blazing through his bloodstream.

In the dark cover of her family terrace and the subsequent helicopter journey home, he'd found relief from the blatant temptation of her body.

In the clear light of day, the red dress seemed to cling tighter, caress her body so much more intimately that he'd had to fight the urge to lunge for her each time she took a breath.

He watched her now, seated across from him in his limo as they drove the short twenty-minute distance to Threadneedle Street where his bankers had flown in the diamond collection he'd requested from Switzerland.

Her fingers plucked at the lapel of the new white cashmere coat, then dropped to cinch the belt tighter at her tiny waist.

'You didn't need to buy me a coat,' she grumbled. 'I have a perfectly good one back at my flat.'

He reined in his fascination with her fingers. 'Your flat is on the other side of town. I have more important things to do than waste an hour and a half sitting in traffic.'

Her plump lips pursed. 'Of course, extracting your pound of flesh is an all-consuming business, isn't it?'

'I don't intend to stop at a mere pound, Eva. I intend to take the whole body.'

One eyebrow spiked. 'You seem so confident I'm going to hand myself to you on a silver platter. Isn't that a tad foolish?'

There was that tone again, the one that said she didn't believe him.

'I guess we'll find out one way or the other when the sordid details are laid out for you on Monday. All you need to concern yourself about today is picking out an engagement ring that makes the right statement.'

Her striking green eyes clashed with his and that lightning bolt struck again. 'And what statement would that be?' she challenged.

He let loose a chilling half-smile that made his enemies quake. 'Why, that you belong to me, of course.'

'I told you, I've no intention of being your possession. A ring won't change that.'

'How glibly you lie to yourself.'

She gasped and he was once again drawn to her mouth. A mouth whose sweet taste he recalled vividly, much to his annoyance. 'Excuse me?'

'We both know you'll be exactly who and what I want you to be when I demand it. Your family has too much at stake for you to risk doing otherwise.'

'Don't mistake my inclination to go along with this farce to be anything but my need to get to the bottom of why you're doing this. It's what families *do* for each other. Of course, since you don't even speak about yours, I assume you don't know what I'm talking about.'

Zaccheo called himself ten kinds of fool for letting the taunt bite deep. He'd lost respect for his father long before he'd died in shame and humiliation. And watching his mother whore herself for prestige had left a bitter taste in his mouth. As families went, he'd been dealt a bad hand, but he'd learned long ago that to wish for anything you couldn't create with your own hard-working hands was utter folly. He'd stopped making wishes by the time he hit puberty. Recalling the very last wish he'd prayed night and day for as a child, he clenched his fists. Even then he'd known fate would laugh at his wish for a brother or sister. He'd known that wish, despite his mother being pregnant, would not come true. He'd *known*.

He'd programmed himself not to care after that harrowing time in his life.

So why the hell did it grate so much for him to be reminded that he was the last Giordano?

'I don't talk about my family because I have none. But that's a situation I intend to rectify soon.'

She glanced at him warily. 'What's that supposed to mean?'

'It means I had a lot of time in prison to re-examine my life, thanks to your family.' He heard the naked emotion in his voice and hardened his tone. 'I intend to make some changes.'

'What sort of changes?'

'The type that means you'll no longer have to whore out your integrity for the sake of the great Pennington legacy. You should thank me, since you seem to be the one doing most of the heavy lifting for your family.'

Zaccheo watched her face pale.

'I'm not a whore!'

He lunged forward before he could stop himself. 'Then what the hell were you doing dressed like a tart, agreeing to marry a drunken playboy, if not for cold, hard cash for your family?' The reminder of what she wore beneath the coat blazed across his mind. His temperature hiked, along with the increased throbbing in his groin.

'I didn't do it for money!' She flushed, and bit down on her lower lip again. 'Okay, yes, that was part of the reason, but I also did it because—'

'Please spare me any declarations of *true love*.' He wasn't sure why he abhorred the idea of her mentioning the word love. Or why the idea of her mentioning Fairfield's name filled him with rage.

Zaccheo knew about her friendship with Fairfield. And while he knew their engagement had been a farce, he hadn't missed the camaraderie between them, or the pathetic infatuation in the other man's eyes.

Sì, he was jealous—Eva would be his and no one else's. But he also pitied Fairfield.

Because love, in all forms, was a false emotion. Nothing but a manipulative tool. Mothers declared their love for their children, then happily abandoned them the moment they ceased to be a convenient accessory. Fathers professed to have their children's interest at heart because of *love*, but when it came right down to it they put themselves above all else. And sometimes even forgot that their children *existed*.

As for Eva Pennington, she'd shown how faithless she was when she'd dropped him and distanced herself mere days before his arrest.

'I wasn't going to say that. Trust me, I've learned not to toss the word *love* about freely—'

'Did you know?' he sliced at her before he could stop himself.

Fine brows knitted together. 'Did I know what?'

'Did you know of your father's plans?' The question had been eating at him far more than he wanted to admit.

'His plans to do what?' she asked innocently. And yet he could see the caginess on her face. As if she didn't want him to probe deeper.

Acrid disappointment bit through him. He was a fool for thinking, perhaps *wishing*, despite all the signs saying otherwise, that she'd been oblivious to Oscar Pennington's plans to make him the ultimate scapegoat.

'We're here, sir.' His driver's voice came through the intercom.

Zaccheo watched her dive for the door. He would've laughed at her eagerness to get away from the conversation that brought back too many volatile memories, had he not felt disconcerting relief that his question had gone unanswered.

He'd been a fool to pursue it in the first place. He didn't need more lies. He had cold, hard facts proving the Penningtons' guilt. Dwelling on the whys and wherefores of Eva's actions was a fool's errand.

He stepped out into the winter sunshine and nodded at the bank director.

'Mr Giordano, welcome.' The older man's expression vacillated between obsequiousness and condescension.

'You received my further instructions?' Zaccheo took Eva's arm, ignoring her slight stiffening as he walked her through the doors of the bank.

'Yes, sir. We've adhered to your wishes.' Again he caught the man's assessing gaze.

'I'm pleased to hear it. Otherwise I'm sure there would be other banks who would welcome GWI's business.'

The banker paled. 'That won't be necessary, Mr Giordano. If you'll come with me, the jewellers have everything laid out for you.'

It should've given him great satisfaction that he'd breached the hallowed walls of the centuries-old establishment, that he'd finally succeeded where his own father had tried so hard and failed, giving his life in pursuit of recognition.

But all Zaccheo could hear, could *feel*, was Eva's presence, a reminder of why his satisfaction felt hollow. She was proof that, despite all he'd achieved, he was still regarded as the lowest of the low. A nobody. An expendable patsy who would take any treatment his betters doled out without protest.

We shall see.

They walked down several hallways. After a few minutes, Eva cleared her throat. 'What instructions did you give him?' she asked.

He stared down at her. 'I told him to remove all pink diamonds from the collection and instruct my jewellers that I do not wish to deal with diamonds of that colour in the future.'

'Really? I thought pink diamonds were all the rage these days?'

He shrugged. 'Not for me. Let's call it a personal preference.'

The penny dropped and she tried to pull away from his hold. He refused to let go. 'Are you really that petty?' she asked as they approached a heavy set of oak doors. 'Just because Harry gave me a pink diamond...' Her eyes widened when he caught her shoulders and pinned her against the wall. When she started to struggle, he stepped closer, caging her in with his body.

'You'll refrain from mentioning his name in my presence ever again. Is that understood?' Zaccheo felt his control slipping as her scent tangled with his senses and her curvy figure moved against him.

'Let me go and you'll need never hear his name again,' she snapped back.

'Not going to happen.' He released her. 'After you.'

She huffed a breath and entered the room. He followed and crossed to the window, struggling to get himself under control as the director walked in with three assistants bearing large velvet trays. They set them on the polished conference table and stepped back.

'We'll give you some privacy,' the director said before exiting with his minions.

Zaccheo walked to the first tray and pulled away the protective cloth. He stared at the display of diamonds in all cuts and sizes, wondering for a moment how his father would've reacted to this display of obscene wealth. Paolo Giordano had never managed to achieve even a fraction of his goals despite sacrificing everything, including the people he should've held dear. Would he have been proud, or would he have bowed and scraped as the bank director had a few moments ago, eager to be deemed worthy of merely touching them?

'Perhaps we should get on with choosing a stone. Or are we going to stare at them all day?' Eva asked.

Eva watched his face harden and bit her tongue. She wasn't sure why she couldn't stop goading him. Did part of her want to get under his skin as he so effortlessly got under hers?

Annoyed with herself for letting the whole absurd situation get to her, she stepped forward and stared down at the dazzling array of gems. Large. Sparkling. Flawless. Each worth more than she would earn in half her lifetime.

None of them appealed to her.

She didn't want to pick out another cold stone to replace the one she'd handed back to Harry before running after Zaccheo last night.

She didn't want to be trapped into yet another consequence of being a Pennington. She wanted to be free of the guilty resentment lurking in her heart at the thought that nothing she did would ever be enough for her family. Or the sadness that came with the insurmountable knowledge that her sister would continue to block any attempt to forge a relationship with her father.

She especially didn't want to be trapped in any way with Zaccheo Giordano. That display of his displeasure a few moments ago had reminded her she wanted nothing to do with him. And it was not about his temper but what she'd felt when her body had been thrust against his. She'd wanted to be held there...indefinitely.

Touching him.

Soothing his angry brow and those brief flashes of pain she saw in his eyes when he thought she wasn't looking.

God, even a part of her wanted to coax out that heart-stopping smile she'd glimpsed so very rarely when he was pursuing her!

What was wrong with her?

'Is that the one you wish for?'

She jumped and stared down at the stone that had somehow found its way into her palm. She blinked in shock.

The diamond was the largest on the tray and twice as obscene as the one that had graced her finger last night. No wonder Zaccheo sounded so disparaging.

'No!' She hastily dropped it back into its slot. 'I'd never wear anything so gratuitous.'

His coldly mocking gaze made her cringe. 'Really?'

Irritation skated over her skin. 'For your information, I didn't choose that ring.'

'But you accepted it in the spirit it was given—as the cost of buying your body in exchange for shares in Penningtons?'

Icy rage replaced her irritation. 'Your continuous insults make me wonder why you want to put up with my presence. Surely revenge can't be as sweet as you wish it if the object of your punishment enrages you this much?'

'Perhaps I enjoy tormenting you.'

'So I'm to be your punching bag for the foreseeable future?'

'Is this your way of trying to find out how long your sentence is to be?'

'A sentence implies I've done something wrong. I *know* I'm innocent in whatever you believe I've done.'

His smile could've turned a volcano into a polar ice cap. 'I've found that proclamations of innocence don't count for a thing, not when the right palm is greased.'

She inhaled at the fury and bitterness behind his words. 'Zaccheo…'

Whatever feeble reply she'd wanted to make died when his eyes hardened.

'Choose the diamond you prefer or I'll choose it for you.'

Eva turned blindly towards the table and pointed to the smallest stone. 'That one.'

'No.'

She gritted her teeth. 'Why not?'

'Because it's pink.'

'No, it's not…' She leaned closer, caught the faint pink glow, and frowned. 'Oh. I thought—'

A mirthless smile touched his lips. 'So did I. Perhaps I'll change bankers after all.' He lifted the cover of the second tray and Eva stared dispassionately at the endless rows of sparkling jewels. None of them spoke to her. Her heart hammered as it finally dawned on her why.

'Is there any reason why you want to buy me a new ring?'

He frowned. *'Scusi?'*

'When you proposed the first time, you gave me a different ring. I'm wondering why you're buying me a different one. Did you lose it?' Despite the circumstances surrounding his proposal and her subsequent rejection of him, she'd loved that simple but exquisite diamond and sapphire ring.

'No, I didn't lose it.' His tone was clipped to the point of brusqueness.

'Then why?'

'Because I do not wish you to have it.'

Her heart did an achy little dance as she waited for further elaboration. When she realised none would be forthcoming, she pulled her gaze from his merciless regard and back to the display.

He didn't want her to have it. Why? Because the ring held special meaning? Or because she was no longer worthy of it?

Berating herself for feeling hurt, she plucked a stone from the middle of the tray. According to the size chart it sat in mid-range, a flawless two carat, square-cut that felt light in her palm. 'This one.' She turned and found him staring at her, his gaze intense yet inscrutable.

Wordlessly, he held out his hand.

Her fingers brushed his palm as she dropped the stone and she bit back a gasp as that infernal electricity zinged up her arm.

His eyes held hers for a long moment before he turned and headed for the door. The next few minutes passed in a blur as Zaccheo issued clipped instructions about mountings, scrolls and settings to the jeweller.

Before she could catch her breath, Eva was back outside. Flashes went off as a group of paparazzi lunged towards them. Zaccheo handed her into the car before joining her. With a curt instruction to the driver, the car lurched into traffic.

'If I've achieved my publicity quota for the day, I'd like to be dropped at my flat, please.'

Zaccheo focused those incisive eyes on her. 'Why would I do that?'

'Aren't we done? I'd catch a bus home, but I left my handbag and phone at Pennington Manor—'

'Your belongings have been brought to my penthouse,' he replied.

'Okay, thanks. As soon as I collect them, I'll be out of your hair.' She needed to get out of this dress, shower and practise the six songs she would be performing at the club tonight. Saturday nights were the busiest of the week, and she couldn't be late. The music producer who'd been frequenting the club for the last few weeks might make another appearance tonight.

A little bubble of excitement built and she squashed it down as that half-smile that chilled her to the bone appeared on Zaccheo's face.

'You misunderstand. When I mentioned your belongings, I didn't mean your handbag and your phone. I meant everything you own in your bedsit has been removed. While we were picking your engagement ring, your belongings were relocated. Your rent has been paid off with interest and your landlady is busy renting the property to someone else.'

'What on earth are you talking about?' she finally asked when she'd picked up her jaw from the floor and sifted through his words. 'Of course I still live there. Mrs Hammond wouldn't just let you into my flat. And she certainly wouldn't arbitrarily end my lease without speaking to me first.'

Zaccheo just stared back at her.

'How dare you? Did you threaten her?'

'No, Eva. I used a much more effective tool.'

Her mouth twisted. 'You mean you threw so much money at her she buckled under your wishes?'

He shrugged rugged, broad shoulders. 'You of all people

should know how money sways even the most veracious hearts. Mrs Hammond was thrilled at the prospect of receiving her new hip replacement next week instead of at the end of the year. But it also helps that she's a hopeless romantic. The picture of us in the paper swayed any lingering doubts she had.'

Eva's breath shuddered out. Her landlady had lamented the long waiting list over shared cups of tea and Eva had offered a sympathetic ear. While she was happy that Mrs Hammond would receive her treatment earlier than anticipated and finally be out of pain, a huge part of her couldn't see beyond the fact that Zaccheo had ripped her safe harbour away without so much as a by your leave.

'You had absolutely no right to do that,' she blazed at him.

'Did I not?' he asked laconically.

'No, you didn't. This is nothing but a crude demonstration of your power. Well, guess what, I'm unimpressed. Go ahead and do your worst! Whatever crimes you think we've committed, maybe going to prison is a better option than this…this kidnapping!'

'Believe me, prison isn't an option you want to joke with.'

His lacerated tone made her heart lurch. She looked into his face and saw the agony. Her eyes widened, stunned that he was letting her witness that naked emotion.

'You think you know what it feels like to be robbed of your freedom for months on end? Pray you never get to find out, Eva. Because you may not survive it.'

'Zaccheo… I…' She stuttered to a halt, unsure of what to make of that raw statement.

His hand slashed through the air and his mask slid back into place. 'I wanted you relocated as swiftly as possible with a minimum of fuss,' he said.

A new wave of apprehension washed over her. 'Why? What's the rush?'

'I thought that would be obvious, Eva. I have deep-seated trust issues.'

Sadly, she'd reaped the rewards of betrayed trust, but the fierce loyalty to her family that continued to burn within her made her challenge him. 'How is that my family's fault?'

His nostrils flared. 'I trusted your father. He repaid that trust with a betrayal that sent me to prison! And you were right there next to him.'

Again she heard the ragged anguish in his voice. A hysterical part of her mind wondered whether this was the equivalent of a captor revealing his face to his prisoner. Was she doomed now that she'd caught a glimpse of what Zaccheo's imprisonment had done to him?

'So you keeping me against my will is meant to be part of *my* punishment?'

He smiled. 'You don't have to stay. You have many options available to you. You can call the police, tell them I'm holding you against your will, although that would be hard to prove since three hundred people saw you chase after me last night. Or you can insist I return your things and reinstate your lease. If you choose to walk away, no one will lift a finger to stop you.'

'But that's not quite true, is it? What real choice do I have when you're holding a threat over my father's head?'

'Leave him to flounder on his own if you truly believe you're guilt-free in all of this. You want to make a run for it? Here's your chance.'

His pointed gaze went to the door and Eva realised they'd completed the short journey from the bank to the iconic building that had brought Zaccheo into her life and turned it upside down.

She glanced up at the building *Architectural Digest* had called 'innovative beyond its years' and 'a heartbreakingly beautiful masterpiece'.

Where most modern buildings boasted elaborate glass edifices, The Spire was a study in polished, tensile steel. Thin sheets of steel had been twisted and manipulated around the towering spear-like structure, making the tallest building in

London a testament to its architect's skill and innovation. Its crowning glory was its diamond-shaped, vertiginous platform, within which was housed a Michelin-starred restaurant surrounded by a clear twenty-foot waterfall.

One floor beneath the restaurant was Zaccheo's penthouse. Her new home. Her prison.

The sound of him exiting the car drew her attention. When he held out his hand to her, she hesitated, unable to accept that this was her fate.

A muscle ticced in his jaw as he waited.

'You'd love that, wouldn't you? Me helping you bury my father?'

'He's going down either way. It's up to you whether he gets back up or not.'

Eva wanted to call his bluff. To shut the door and return everything to the way it was this time yesterday.

The memory of her father in that hospital bed, strung up to a beeping machine, stopped her. She'd already lost one parent. No matter how difficult things were between them, she couldn't bear to lose another. She would certainly have no hope of saving her relationship with her sister if she walked away.

Because one thing was certain. Zaccheo meant to have his way.

With or without her co-operation.

CHAPTER SIX

EVA BLEW HER fringe out of her eyes and glanced around her. The guest suite, a different one from the one she'd slept in last night, was almost three times the size of her former bedsit. And every surface was covered with designer gowns and accessories. Countless bottles of exclusive perfumes and luxury grooming products were spread on the dresser, and a team of six stylists each held an item of clothing, ready to pounce on her the moment she took off the dress she was currently trying on.

She tried hard to see the bright side of finally being out of the red dress. Unfortunately, any hint of brightness had vanished the moment she'd stepped out of the car and re-entered Zaccheo's penthouse.

'How many more before we're done?' She tried to keep her voice even, but she knew she'd missed amiability by a mile when two assistants exchanged wary glances.

'We've done your home and evening-wear package. We just need to do your vacation package and we'll be done with wardrobe. Then we can move on to hair and make-up,' Vivian, the chief stylist, said with a megawatt smile.

Eva tried not to groan. She needed to be done so she could find her phone and call her father. There was no way she was twiddling her thumbs until Monday to get a proper answer.

Being made into Zaccheo's revenge punchbag...his *married* revenge punchbag...wasn't a role she intended to be placed in. When she'd thought there was a glimmer of doubt as to Zaccheo's threat being real, she'd gone along with this farce. But with each hour that passed with silence from her father, Eva was forced to believe Zaccheo's threats weren't empty.

Would he go to such lengths to have her choose precious gems, remove her from her flat, and hire a team of stylists to turn her into the sort of woman he preferred to date, if this was just some sort of twisted game?

Her hand clenched as her thoughts took a different path. What exactly was Zaccheo trying to turn her into? Obviously he wasn't just satisfied with attaining her pedigree for whatever his nefarious purposes were. He wanted her to look like a well-dressed mannequin while he was at it.

'Careful with that, Mrs Giordano. That lace is delicate.'

She dropped the dress, her heart hammering far too fast for her liking. 'Don't call me that. I'm not Mrs Giordano—'

'Not yet, at least, right, *bellissima*?'

Eva heard the collective breaths of the women in the room catch. She turned as Zaccheo strode in. His eyes were fixed on her, flashing a warning that made her nape tingle. Before she could respond, he lifted her hands to kiss her knuckles, one after the other. Her breathing altered precariously as the silky hairs of his beard and the warm caress of his mouth threw her thoughts into chaos.

'It's only a few short days until we're husband and wife, *si*?' he murmured intimately, but loud enough so every ear in the room caught the unmistakeable statement of possession.

She struggled to think, to *speak*, as sharp grey eyes locked with hers.

'No…I mean, yes…but let's not tempt fate. Who knows what could happen in a *few short days*?' She fully intended to have placed this nightmare far behind her.

His thumbs caressed the backs of her hands in false intimacy. 'I've moved mountains to make you mine, *il mio prezioso*. Nothing will stand in my way.' His accent was slightly more pronounced, his tone deep and captivating.

Envious sighs echoed around the room, but Eva shivered at the icy intent behind his words. She snatched her hands from his. Or she attempted to.

'In that case, I think you ought to stop distracting me so I can get on with making myself beautiful for you.' She hoped her smile looked as brittle as it felt. That her intention to end this was clear for him to see. 'Or was there something in particular you wanted?'

His eyes held hers for another electrifying second before he released her. 'I came to inform you that your belongings have been unpacked.' He surveyed the room, his gaze taking in the organised chaos. 'And to enquire whether you wish to have lunch with me or whether you want lunch brought to you so you can push through?' He turned back to her, his gaze mockingly stating that he knew her choice before she responded.

She lifted her chin. 'Seeing as this makeover was a complete *surprise* that I'd have to *make* time for, we'll take lunch in here, please.'

He ignored her censorious tone and nodded. 'Your wish is my command, *dolcezza*. But I insist you be done by dinnertime. I detest eating alone.'

She bit her tongue against a sharp retort. The cheek of him, making demands on her time when *he'd* been the one to call in the stylists in the first place! She satisfied herself with glaring at his back as he walked out, his tall, imposing figure owning every square inch of space he prowled.

The women left three excruciating hours later. The weak sun was setting in grey skies by the time Eva dragged her weary body across the vast hallway towards the suite she'd occupied last night. Her newly washed and styled hair bounced in silky waves down her back and her face tingled pleasantly from the facial she'd received before the barely there make-up had been applied.

The cashmere-soft, scooped-neck grey dress caressed her hips and thighs as she approached her door. She'd worn it only because Vivian had insisted. Eva hadn't had the heart to tell her she intended to leave every single item untouched. But Eva couldn't deny that the off-shoulder, floor-length dress felt elegant and wonderful and exactly what she'd have chosen to wear for dinner. Even if it was a dinner she wasn't looking forward to.

Her new four-inch heels clicked on the marble floor as she opened the double doors and stopped. Her hands flew to cover her mouth as she surveyed the room. Surprise was followed a few seconds later by a tingle of awareness that told her she was no longer alone.

Even then, she couldn't look away from the sight before her.

'Is something wrong?' Zaccheo's enquiry made her finally turn.

He was leaning against the door frame, his hands tucked into the pockets of his black tailored trousers. The white V-necked sweater caressed his muscular arms and shoulders and made his grey eyes appear lighter, almost eerily silver. His slightly damp hair gleamed a polished black against his shoulders and his beard lent him a rakish look that was absolutely riveting.

His gaze caught and held hers for several seconds before conducting a detailed appraisal over her face, hair and down her body that made the tingling increase. When his eyes returned to hers, she glimpsed a dark hunger that made her insides quake.

Swallowing against the pulse of undeniable attraction, she turned back to survey the room.

'I can't believe everything's been arranged so precisely,' she murmured.

'You would've preferred that they fling your things around without thought or care?'

'That's not what I mean and you know it. You've reproduced my room almost exactly how it was before.'

He frowned. 'I fail to see how that causes you distress.'

She strolled to the white oak antique dresser that had belonged to her mother. It'd been her mother's favourite piece of furniture and one of the few things Eva had taken when she'd left Pennington Manor.

Her fingers drifted over the hairbrush she'd used only yesterday morning. It had been placed in the little stand just as she normally did. 'I'm not distressed. I'm a little disconcerted that my things are almost exactly as I left them at my flat yesterday morning.' When he continued to stare, she pursed her lips. 'To reproduce this the movers would've needed photographic memories.'

'Or a few cameras shots as per my instructions.'

She sucked in a startled breath. 'Why would you do that?'

His lashes swept down for a moment. Then he shrugged. 'It was the most efficient course of action.'

'Oh.' Eva wasn't sure why she experienced that bolt of disappointment. Was she stupid enough to believe he'd done that because he *cared*? That he'd wanted her to be comfortable?

She silently scoffed at herself.

Lending silly daydreams to Zaccheo's actions had led to bitter disappointment once before. She wasn't about to make the same mistake again.

She spotted her handbag on the bed and dug out her phone. The battery was almost depleted, but she could make a quick call to her father before it died. She started to press dial and realised Zaccheo hadn't moved.

'Did you need something?'

The corner of his mouth quirked, but the bleakness in his eyes didn't dissipate. 'I've been in jail for over a year, *dolcezza*. I have innumerable needs.' The soft words held a note of deadly intent as his gaze moved from her to the bed. Her heart jumped to her throat and the air seemed to evaporate from the room. 'But my most immediate need is sustenance. I've ordered dinner to be brought from upstairs. It'll be here in fifteen minutes.'

She managed to reply despite the light-headedness that assailed her. 'Okay. I'll be there.'

With a curt nod, he left.

Eva sagged sideways onto the bed, her grip on the phone tightening until her bones protested. In the brief weeks she'd dated Zaccheo a year and half ago, she'd seen the way women responded to his unmistakeable animal magnetism. He only needed to walk into the room for every female eye to zero in on him. She'd also witnessed his reaction. Sometimes he responded with charm, other times with arrogant aloofness. But always with an innate sexuality that spoke of a deep appreciation for women. She'd confirmed that appreciation by a quick internet search in a weak moment, which had unearthed the long list of gorgeous women he'd had shockingly brief liaisons with in the past. A young, virile, wealthy bachelor, he'd been at the top of every woman's 'want to bed' list. And he'd had no qualms about helping himself to their amorous attentions.

To be deprived of that for almost a year and a half...

Eva shivered despite the room's ambient temperature. No, she was the last woman Zaccheo would *choose* to bed.

But then, he'd kissed her last night as if he'd wanted to devour her. And the way he'd looked at her just now?

She shook her head.

She was here purely as an instrument of his vengeance. The quicker she got to the bottom of *that*, the better.

Her call went straight to voicemail. Gritting her teeth, she left a message for her father to call her back. Sophie's phone rang for almost a minute before Eva hung up. Whether her sister was deliberately avoiding her calls or not, Eva intended to get some answers before Monday.

Resolving to try again after dinner, Eva plugged in her phone to charge and left her room. She met two waiters wheeling out a trolley as she entered the dining room. A few seconds later, the front door shut and Eva fought the momentary panic at being alone with Zaccheo.

She avoided looking at his imposing body as he lifted the silver domes from several serving platters.

'You always were impeccably punctual,' he said without turning around.

'I suppose that's a plus in my favour.'

'Hmm...' came his non-committal reply.

She reached her seat and froze at the romantic setting of the table. Expensive silverware and crystal-cut glasses gleamed beneath soft lighting. And already set out in a bed of ice was a small silver tub of caviar. A bottle of champagne chilled in an ice stand next to Zaccheo's chair.

'Do you intend to eat standing up?'

She jumped when his warm breath brushed her ear. When had he moved so close?

'Of course not. I just wasn't expecting such an elaborate meal.' She urged her feet to move to where he held out her chair, and sat down. 'One would almost be forgiven for thinking you were celebrating something.'

'Being released from prison isn't reason enough to enjoy something better than grey slop?'

Mortified, she cursed her tactlessness. 'I...of course. I'm sorry, that was... I'd forgotten...' *Oh, God, just shut up, Eva.*

'Of course you had.'

She tensed. 'What's that supposed to mean?'

'You're very good at putting things behind you, aren't you? Or have you forgotten how quickly you walked away from me the last time, too?'

She glanced down at her plate, resolutely picked up her spoon and helped herself to a bite of caviar. The unique taste exploded on her tongue, but it wasn't enough to quell the anxiety churning her stomach. 'You know why I walked away last time.'

'Do I?'

'Yes, you do!' She struggled to keep her composure. 'Can we talk about something else, please?'

'Why, because your actions make you uncomfortable? Or does it make your skin crawl to be sharing a meal with an ex-convict?'

Telling herself not to rise to the bait, she took another bite of food. 'No, because you snarl and your voice turns arctic, and also because I think we have different definitions of what really happened.'

He helped himself to a portion of his caviar before he responded. 'Really? Enlighten me, *per favore.*'

She pressed her lips together. 'We've already been through this, remember? You admitted that you proposed to me simply to get yourself into the Old Boys' Club. Are you going to bother denying it now?'

He froze for several heartbeats. Then he ate another mouthful. 'Of course not. But I believed we had an agreement. That you knew the part you had to play.'

'I'm sorry, I must have misplaced my copy of the Zaccheo Giordano Relationship Guide.' She couldn't stem the sarcasm or the bitterness that laced her voice.

'You surprise me.'

'How so?' she snapped, her poise shredding by the second.

'You're determined to deny that you know exactly how this game is played. That you aristocrats haven't practised the *something-for-something-more* tenet for generations.'

'You seem to be morbidly fascinated with the inner workings of the peer class. If we disgust you so much, why do you insist on soiling your life with our presence? Isn't it a bit convenient to hold us all responsible for every ill in your life?'

A muscle ticced in his jaw and Eva was certain she'd struck a nerve. 'You think having my freedom taken away is a subject I should treat lightly?'

The trembling in her belly spread out to engulf her whole body. 'The *evidence* led to your imprisonment, Zaccheo. Now we can change the subject or we can continue to fight to see who gives whom indigestion first.'

He remained silent for several moments, his eyes boring into hers. Eva stared back boldly, because backing down would see her swallowed whole by the deadly volcanic fury lurking in his eyes. She breathed a tiny sigh of relief when that mocking half-smile made an appearance.

'As you wish.' He resumed eating and didn't speak again until their first course was done. 'Let's play a game. We'll call it *What If*,' he said into the silence.

Tension knotted her nape, the certainty that she was toying with danger rising higher. 'I thought you didn't like games?'

'I'll make an exception this time.'

She took a deep breath. 'Okay. If you insist.'

'What if I wasn't the man you think I am? What if I happened to be a stranger who was innocent of everything he's been accused of? What if that stranger told you that every day he'd spent in prison felt like a little bit of himself was being chipped away for ever? What would you say to him?' His voice held that pain-laced edge she'd first heard in the car.

She looked at his face but his eyes were downcast, his white-knuckled hand wrapped around his wine glass.

This was no game.

The tension that gripped her vibrated from him, engulfing them in a volatile little bubble.

'I'd tell you how sorry I was that justice wasn't served properly on your behalf.' Her voice shook but she held firm. 'Then I'd ask you if there was anything I could do to help you put the past behind you.'

Arctic grey eyes met hers. 'What if I didn't want to put it behind me? What if everything I believe in tells me the only way to achieve satisfaction is to make those responsible pay?'

'I'd tell you it may seem like a good course of action, but doing that won't get back what you've lost. I'd also ask why you thought that was the only way.'

His eyes darkened, partly in anger, partly with anguish. She half expected him to snarl at her for daring to dissuade him from his path of retribution.

Instead, he rose and went to dish out their second course. 'Perhaps I don't know another recourse besides crime and punishment?' he intoned, disturbingly calm.

Sorrow seared her chest. 'How can that be?'

He returned with their plates and set down her second course—a lobster thermidor—before taking his seat. His movements were jerky, lacking his usual innate grace.

'Let's say hypothetically that I've never been exposed to much else.'

'But you know better or you wouldn't be so devastated at the hand you've been dealt. You're angry, yes, but you're also wounded by your ordeal. Believe me, yours isn't a unique story, Zaccheo.'

He frowned at the naked bitterness that leaked through her voice. 'Isn't it? Enlighten me. How have *you* been wounded?'

She cursed herself for leaving the door open, but, while she couldn't backtrack, she didn't want to provide him with more ammunition against her. 'My family...we're united where it counts, but I've always had to earn whatever regard I receive, especially from my father. And it hasn't always been easy, especially when walls are thrown up and alliances built where there should be none.'

He saw through her vagueness immediately. 'Your father and your sister against your mother and you? There's no need to deny it. It's easy to see your sister is fashioning herself in the image of her father,' he said less than gently.

Eva affected an easy shrug. 'Father started grooming her when we were young, and I didn't mind. I just didn't understand why that meant being left out in the cold, especially...' She stopped, realising just how much she was divulging.

'Especially...?' he pressed.

She gripped her fork tighter. 'After my mother died. I thought things would be different. I was wrong.'

His mouth twisted. 'Death is supposed to be a profound leveller. But it rarely changes people.'

She looked at him. 'Your parents—'

'Were the individuals who brought me into the world. They weren't good for much else. Take from that what you will. We're also straying away from the subject. *What if* this stranger can't see his way to forgive and forget?' That ruth-less edge was back in his voice.

Eva's hand shook as she picked up her glass of Chianti. 'Then he needs to ask himself if he's prepared to live with the consequences of his actions.'

His eyebrows locked together in a dark frown, before his lashes swept down and he gave a brisk nod. 'Asked and an-swered.'

'Then there's no further point to this game, is there?'

One corner of his mouth lifted. 'On the contrary, you've shown a soft-heartedness that some would see as a flaw.'

Eva released a slow, unsteady breath. Had he always been like this? She was ashamed to admit she'd been so dazzled with Zaccheo from the moment he'd walked into Siren two years ago, right until the day he'd shown her his true colours, that she hadn't bothered to look any deeper. He'd kissed her on their third date, after which, fearing she'd disappoint him, she'd stumblingly informed him she was a virgin.

His reaction had been something of a fairy tale for her. She'd made him out as her Prince Charming, had adored the way he'd treated her like a treasured princess, showering her with small, thoughtful gifts, but, most of all, his undivided time whenever they were together. He'd made her feel pre-cious, adored. He'd proposed on their sixth date, which had coincided with his thirtieth birthday, and told her he wanted to spend the rest of his life with her.

And it had all been a lie. The man sitting in front of her had no softness, only that ruthless edge and deadly charm.

'Don't be so sure, Zaccheo. I've learnt a few lessons since our unfortunate association.'

'Like what?'

'I'm no longer gullible. And my family may not be per-fect, but I'm still fiercely protective of those I care about. Don't forget that.'

He helped himself to his wine. 'Duly noted.' His almost

bored tone didn't fool her into thinking this subject had stopped being anything but volatile.

They finished their meal in tense silence.

Eva almost wilted in relief when the doorbell rang and Zaccheo walked away to answer it.

Catching sight of the time, she jumped up from the dining table and was crossing the living room when Zaccheo's hand closed over her wrist.

'Where do you think you're going?' he demanded.

'Dinner's over. Can you let me go, please? I need to get going or I'll be late.'

His brows furrowed, giving him a look of a dark predator. 'Late for what?'

'Late for work. I've already taken two days off without pay. I don't want to be late on top of everything else.'

'You still work at Siren?' His tone held a note of disbelief.

'I have to make a living, Zaccheo.'

'You still sing?' His voice had grown deeper, his eyes darkening to a molten grey as he stared down at her. Although Zaccheo's expression could be hard to decipher most of the time, the mercurial changes in his eyes often spelled his altered mood.

This molten grey was one she was familiar with. And even though she didn't want to be reminded of it, a pulse of decadent sensation licked through her belly as she recalled the first night she'd seen him.

He'd walked into Siren an hour before closing, when she'd been halfway through a sultry, soulful ballad—a song about forbidden love, stolen nights and throwing caution to the wind. He'd paused to order a drink at the bar, then made his way to the table directly in front of the stage. He'd sipped his whisky, not once taking his eyes off her. Every lyric in the three songs that had followed had felt as if it had been written for the man in front of her and the woman she'd wanted to be for him.

She'd been beyond mesmerised when he'd helped her off

the stage after her session. She'd said yes immediately when he'd asked her out the next night.

But she'd been wrong, so very wrong to believe fate had brought Zaccheo to the club. He'd hunted her down with single-minded intent for his own selfish ends.

God, how he must have laughed when she'd fallen so easily into his arms!

She yanked her arm free. 'Yes, I still sing. And I'd be careful before you start making any threats on my professional life, too. I've indulged you with the engagement-ring picking and the makeover and the homecoming dinner. Now I intend to get back to *my* reality.'

She hurried away, determined not to look over her shoulder to see whether he was following. She made it to her room and quickly changed into her going-to-work attire of jeans, sweater, coat and a thick scarf to ward off the winter chill. Scooping up her bag, she checked her phone.

No calls.

The unease in her belly ballooned as she left her suite.

Zaccheo was seated on the sofa in the living room, examining a small black velvet box. His eyes tracked her, inducing that feeling of being helpless prey before a ruthless marauder. She opened her mouth to say something to dispel the sensation, but no words emerged. She watched, almost paralysingly daunted as he shut the box and placed it on the coffee table next to him.

'Would it be too *indulgent* to demand a kiss before you leave for work, *dolcezza*?' he enquired mockingly.

'Indulgent, no. Completely out of the question, most definitely,' she retorted. Then silently cursed her mouth's sudden tingling.

He shook his head, his magnificent mane gleaming under the chandelier. 'You wound me, Eva, but I'm willing to wait until the time when you will kiss me freely without me needing to ask.'

'Then you'll be waiting an eternity.'

CHAPTER SEVEN

ZACCHEO PACED THE living room and contemplated leaving another voicemail message.

He'd already left five, none of which Eva had bothered to answer. It was nearly two a.m. and she hadn't returned. In his gloomy mood, he'd indulged in one too many nightcaps to consider driving to the club where she worked.

His temperament had been darkening steadily for the last four hours, once he'd found out what Eva's father was up to. Pennington was scrambling—futilely of course, because Zaccheo had closed every possible avenue—to find financial backing. That was enough to anger Zaccheo, but what fuelled his rage was that Pennington, getting more desperate by the hour, was offering more and more pieces of The Spire, the building that he would no longer own come Monday, as collateral. The blatant fraud Pennington was willing to perpetrate to fund his lifestyle made Zaccheo's fists clench as he stalked to the window.

The view from The Spire captured the string of bridges from east to west London. The moment he'd brought his vision of the building to life with the help of his experienced architects had been one of the proudest moments of his life. More than the properties he owned across the world and the empire he'd built from the first run-down warehouse he'd bought and converted to luxury accommodation at the age of twenty, this had been the one he'd treasured most. The building that should've been his crowning glory.

Instead it'd become the symbol of his downfall.

Ironically, the court where he'd been sentenced was right across the street. He looked down at the courthouse, jaw clenched.

He intended it to be the same place where his name was cleared. He would not be broken and humiliated as his father had been by the time he'd died. He would not be whispered about behind his back and mocked to his face and called a parasite. Earlier this evening, Eva had demanded to know why he'd been so fascinated with her kind.

For a moment, he'd wondered whether his burning desire to prove they were not better than him was a weakness. One he should *put behind him*, as Eva had suggested, before he lost a lot more of himself than he already had.

As much as he'd tried he hadn't been able to dismiss her words. Because he'd lied. He knew how to forgive. He'd forgiven his father each time he'd remembered that Zaccheo existed and bothered to take an interest in him. He'd forgiven his mother the first few times she'd let his stepfather treat him like a piece of garbage.

What Zaccheo hadn't told Eva was that he'd eventually learned that forgiveness wasn't effective when the recipient didn't have any use for it.

A weakening emotion like forgiveness would be wasted on Oscar Pennington.

A keycard clicked and he turned as the entry code released the front door.

Sensation very close to relief gut-punched him.

'Where the hell have you been?' He didn't bother to obviate his snarl. Nor could he stop checking her over from head to toe, to ascertain for himself that she wasn't hurt or hadn't been a victim of an accident or a mugging. When he was sure she was unharmed, he snapped his gaze to her face, to be confronted with a quizzical look.

Dio, was she *smirking* at him?

He watched her slide her fingers through her heavy, silky hair and ignored the weariness in the gesture.

'Is it Groundhog Day or something? Because I could've sworn we had a conversation about where I was going earlier this evening.'

He seethed. 'You finished work an hour and a half ago. Where have you been since then?'

She tossed a glare his way before she shrugged off her coat. The sight of the jeans and sweater she'd chosen to wear instead of the roomful of clothes he'd provided further stoked his dark mood.

'How do you know when I finished work?'

'Answer the question, Eva.'

She tugged her handbag from her shoulder and dropped it on the coffee table. Then she kicked off her shoes and pushed up on the balls of her feet in a smooth, practised stretch reminiscent of a ballet dancer.

'I took the night bus. It's cheaper than a cab, but it took forty-five minutes to arrive.'

'*Mi scusi?* You took the *night bus*?' His brain crawled with scenarios that made his blood curdle. He didn't need a spell in prison to be aware of what dangerous elements lurked at night. The thought that Eva had exposed herself, *willingly*, to—

'Careful there, Zaccheo, you almost sound like one of those snobs you detest so much.'

She pushed up again, her feet arching and flattening in a graceful rise and fall.

Despite his blood boiling, he stared, mesmerised, as she completed the stretches. Then he let his gaze drift up her body, knowing he shouldn't, yet unable to stop himself. The sweater, decorated with a D-minor scale motif, hugged her slim torso, emphasising her full, heavy breasts and tiny waist before ending a half-inch above her jeans.

That half-inch of flesh taunted him, calling to mind the smooth warmth of her skin. The simmering awareness that had always existed between them, like a fuse just waiting to be lit, throbbed deep inside. He'd tried to deny it earlier this evening in the hallway, when he'd discovered she still sang at Siren.

He'd tried to erase the sound of her sultry voice, the evocative way Eva Pennington performed on stage. He'd cursed himself when his body had reacted the way it had the very first time he'd heard her sing. That part of his black mood also stemmed from being viscerally opposed to any other man experiencing the same reaction he did from hearing her captivating voice, the way he had been two years ago, was a subject he wasn't willing to acknowledge, never mind tackle.

He pulled his gaze from the alluringly feminine curve of her hips and shapely legs and focused on the question that had been burning through him all night.

'Explain to me how you have two million pounds in your bank account, but take the bus to and from work.'

Her mouth gaped for several seconds before she regained herself. 'How the hell do you know how much money I have in my bank account?' she demanded.

'With the right people with the right skills, very easily. I'm waiting for an answer.'

'You're not going to get one. What I do with my money and how I choose to travel is *my* business.'

'You're wrong, *cara*. As of last night, your welfare is very much my business. And if you think I'm willing to allow you to risk your safety at times when drunken yobs and muggers crawl out of the woodwork, you're very much mistaken.'

'*Allow* me? Next you'll be telling me I need your permission to breathe!'

He spiked his fingers through his hair, wondering if she'd ever been this difficult and he'd somehow missed it. The Eva he remembered, before his eyes had been truly opened to her character, had possessed a quiet passion, not this defiant, wild child before him.

But no, there'd never been anything *child*like about Eva.

She was all woman. His libido had thrilled to it right from the first.

Understandably this acute reaction was because he'd been without a woman for over a year. Now was not the time to let it out of control. The time would arrive soon enough.

She tossed her head in irritation, and the hardening in his groin threatened to prove him wrong.

'Since I need you alive for the foreseeable future, no, you don't require my permission to breathe.'

She had the nerve to roll her eyes. 'Thank you very much!'

'From now on you'll be driven to and from work.'

'No, thanks.'

He gritted his teeth. 'You prefer to spend hours freezing at a bus stop than accept my offer?'

'Yes, because the *offer* comes at a price. I may not know what it is yet, but I've no intention of paying it.'

'Why do you insist on fighting me when we both know you don't have a choice? I'm willing to bet your father didn't return a single one of your phone calls last night.'

Wide, startled eyes met his for a second before she looked away. 'I'm sure he has his reasons.'

It spoke volumes that she didn't deny trying to reach Oscar. 'Reasons more important than answering the phone to his daughter? Do you want to know what he's been up to?'

'I'm sure you're about to apprise me whether I want to hear it or not.'

'He's been calling in every single favour he thinks he's owed. Unfortunately, a man as greedy as your father cashed in most of his favours a long time ago. He's also pleading and begging his way across the country in a bid to save himself from the hole he knows I'm about to bury him in. He didn't take your calls, but he took mine. I recorded it if you wish me to play it back to you?'

Her fists clenched. 'Go to hell, Zaccheo,' she threw at him, but he glimpsed the pain in her eyes.

He almost felt sorry for her. Then he remembered her part in all this.

'Come here, Eva,' he murmured.

She eyed him suspiciously. 'Why?'

'Because I have something for you.'

Her gaze dropped to his empty hands before snapping

back to his face. 'There's nothing you have that I could possibly want.'

'If you make me come over there, I'll take that kiss you owe me from last night.' *Dio*, why had he said that? Now it was all he could think about.

Heat flushed her cheeks. 'I don't owe you a thing. And I certainly don't owe you any kisses.'

The women he'd dated in the past would've fallen over themselves to receive any gift he chose to bestow on them, especially the one he'd tucked into his back pocket.

Slowly, he walked towards her. He made sure his intent was clear. The moment she realised, her hands shot out. 'Stop! Didn't your mother teach you about the honey versus vinegar technique?'

Bitterness drenched him. 'No. My mother was too busy climbing the social ladder after my father died to bother with me. When he was alive, she wasn't much use either.'

She sucked in a shocked breath and concern furrowed her brow. 'I'm sorry.'

Zaccheo rejected the concern and let the sound of her husky voice, scratchy from the vocal strain that came with singing, wash over him instead. He didn't want her concern. But the sex he could deal with.

The need he'd been trying to keep under tight control threatened to snap. He took another step.

'Okay! I'm coming.' She walked barefooted to him. 'I've done as you asked. Give me whatever it is you want to give me.'

'It's in my back pocket.'

She inhaled sharply. 'Is this another of your games, Zaccheo?'

'It'll only take a minute to find out. Are you brave enough, *dolcezza*?' he asked.

Her gaze dropped and he immediately tilted her chin up with one finger. 'Look at me. I want to see your face.'

She blinked, then gathered herself in that way he'd al-

ways found fascinating. Slowly, she reached an arm around
him. Her fingers probed until she found the pocket opening.

They slipped inside and he suppressed a groan as her fingers caressed him through his trousers. His blood rushed
faster south as she searched futilely.

'It's empty,' she stated with a suspicious glare.

'Try the other one.'

She muttered a dirty word that rumbled right through him.
Her colour deepened when he lifted his eyebrow.

'Let's get this over with.' She searched his right pocket
and stilled when she encountered the box.

'Take it out,' he commanded, then stifled another groan
when her fingers dug into his flesh to remove the velvet box.
It took all the control he could muster not to kiss her when
her lips parted and he glimpsed the tip of her tongue.

During his endless months in prison, he'd wondered
whether he'd overrated the chemistry that existed between
Eva and him. The proof that it was as potent as ever triggered
an incandescent hunger that flooded his loins.

Sì, this part of his revenge that involved Eva in his bed,
being inside her and implanting her with his seed, would be
easy enough and pleasurable enough to achieve.

'I cannot wait to take you on our wedding night. Despite
you no longer being a virgin, I'll thoroughly enjoy making
you mine in every imaginable way possible. By the time I'm
done with you, you'll forget every other man that you dared
to replace me with.'

Her eyelids fluttered and she shivered. But the new, as-
sertive Eva came back with fire. 'A bold assertion. But one,
sadly, we'll both see unproven since there'll be no wedding
or wedding night. And in case I haven't mentioned it, you're
the last man I'd ever welcome in my bed.'

Zaccheo chose not to point out that she still had her hand
in his pocket, or that her fingers were digging more firmly
into his buttock.

Instead, he slid his phone from his front pocket, activated the recording app and hit the replay button.

Despite her earlier assertion that she'd grown a thicker skin, shadows of disbelief and hurt criss-crossed her face as she listened to the short conversation summoning her father to a meeting first thing on Monday. Unlike the night before where Pennington had blustered his way through Zaccheo's accusations, he'd listened in tense silence as Zaccheo had told him he knew what he was up to.

Zaccheo had given him a taster of the contents of the documents proving his innocence and the older man had finally agreed to the meeting. Zaccheo had known he'd won when Pennington had declined to bring his lawyers to verify the documents.

Thick silence filled the room after the recording ended.

'Do you believe me now, Eva? Do you believe that your family has wronged me in the most heinous way and that I intend to exact equal retribution?'

Her nostrils flared and her mouth trembled before she wrenched back control. But despite her composure, a sheen of tears appeared in her eyes, announcing her tumultuous emotion. 'Yes.'

'Take the box out of my pocket.'

She withdrew it. His instructions on the mount and setting had been followed to the letter.

'I intended to give it to you after dinner last night. Not on bended knee, of course. I'm sure you'll agree that once was enough?'

Her eyes darkened, as if he'd hurt her somehow. But of course, that was nonsense. She'd returned his first ring and walked away from him after a brief argument he barely recalled, stating that she didn't wish to be married to *a man like him*.

At the time, Zaccheo had been reeling at his lawyers' news that he was about to be charged with criminal negligence. He hadn't been able to absorb the full impact of Eva's betrayal until weeks later, when he'd already been in prison. His trial had been swift, the result of a young, overeager judge desperate to make a name for himself.

But he'd had over a year to replay the last time he'd seen Eva. In court, sitting next to her father, her face devoid of emotion until Zaccheo's sentence had been read out.

In that moment, he'd fooled himself into thinking she'd experienced a moment of agony on his behalf. He'd murmured her name. She'd looked at him. It was then that he'd seen the contempt.

That single memory cleared his mind of any extraneous feelings. 'Open the box and put on the ring,' he said tersely.

His tone must have conveyed his capricious emotional state. She cracked open the small case and slid on the ring without complaint.

He caught her hand in his and raised it, much as he had on Friday night. But this time, the acute need to rip off the evidence of another man's ownership was replaced by a well of satisfaction. 'You're mine, Eva. Until I decide another fate for you, you'll remain mine. Be sure not to forget that.'

Turning on his heel, he walked away.

Eva woke on Monday morning with a heavy heart and a stone in her gut that announced that her life was about to change for ever. It had started to change the moment she'd heard Zaccheo's recorded conversation with her father, but she'd been too shocked afterwards to decipher what her father's guilt meant for her.

Tired and wrung out, she'd stumbled to bed and fallen into a dreamless sleep, then woken and stumbled her way back to work.

Reality had arrived when she'd exited Siren after her shift to find Zaccheo's driver waiting to bring her back to the penthouse. She'd felt it when Zaccheo had told her to be ready to attend his offices in the morning. She'd felt it when she'd walked into her suite and found every item of clothing she'd tried on Saturday neatly stacked in the floor-to-ceiling shelves in her dressing room.

She felt it now when she lifted her hand to adjust her collar and caught the flash of the diamond ring on her finger. The flawless gem she'd chosen so carelessly had been mounted on a bezel setting, with further diamonds in decreasing sizes set in a platinum ring that fitted her perfectly.

You're mine, Eva. Until I decide another fate for you, you'll remain mine.

She was marrying Zaccheo in less than a week. He'd brought forward the initial two-week deadline by a whole week. She would marry him or her father would be reported to the authorities. He'd delivered that little bombshell last night after dinner. No amount of tossing and turning had altered that reality.

When she'd agreed to marry Harry, she'd known it would be purely a business deal, with zero risk to her emotions.

The idea of attaching herself to Zaccheo, knowing the depth of his contempt for her and his hunger for revenge, was bad enough. That undeniably dangerous chemistry that hovered on the point of exploding in her face when she so much as looked at him...*that* terrified her on an unspeakable level. And not because she was afraid he'd use that against her.

What she'd spent the early hours agonising over was her own helplessness against that inescapable pull.

The only way round it was to keep reminding herself why Zaccheo was doing this. Ultimate retribution and humiliation was his goal. He didn't want anything more from her.

An hour later, she sat across from her father and sister and watched in growing horror as Zaccheo's lawyers listed her father's sins.

Oscar Pennington sat hunched over, his pallor grey and his forehead covered in light sweat. Despite having heard Zaccheo's recording last night, she couldn't believe her father would sink so low.

'How could you do this?' she finally blurted when it got

too much to bear. 'And how the hell did you think you'd get away with it?'

Her father glared at her. 'This isn't the time for histrionics, Eva.'

'And you, Sophie? Did you know about this?' Eva asked her sister.

Sophie glanced at the lawyers before she replied, 'Let's not lose focus on why we're here.'

Anger shot through Eva. 'You mean let's pretend that this isn't really happening? That we're not here because Father *bribed* the builders to take shortcuts and blamed someone else for it? And you accuse me of not living in the real world?'

Sophie's lips pursed, but not before a guilty flush rushed into her face. 'Can we not do this now, please?' Her agitated gaze darted to where Zaccheo sat in lethal silence.

Eva stared at her sister, a mixture of anger and sadness seething within her. She was beginning to think they would never get past whatever was broken between them. And maybe she needed to be more like Zaccheo, and divorce herself from her feelings.

Eva glanced at him and the oxygen leached from her lungs.

God!

On Friday night, his all-black attire had lent him an air of suave but icy deadliness reminiscent of a lead in a mafia movie. Since then his casual attires, although equally formidable in announcing his breathtaking physique, had lulled her into a lesser sense of danger.

This morning, in a dark grey pinstripe suit, teamed with a navy shirt, and precisely knotted silver and blue tie, and his hair and beard newly trimmed, Zaccheo was a magnificent vision to behold.

The bespoke clothes flowed over his sleekly honed muscles and olive skin, each movement drawing attention to his powerfully arresting figure.

It was why more than one female employee had stared in

blatant interest as they'd walked into GWI's headquarters in the City this morning. It was why she'd avoided looking at him since they'd sat down.

But she'd made the mistake of looking now. And as he started to turn his head she *knew* she wouldn't be able to look away.

His gaze locked on her and she read the ruthless, possessive statement of ownership in his eyes even before he opened his mouth to speak. 'Eva has already given me what I want—her word that she's willing to do whatever it takes to make reparations.' His gaze dropped to the ring on her finger before he faced her father. 'Now it's your turn.'

CHAPTER EIGHT

'HERE'S A LIST of businesses who withdrew their contracts because of my incarceration.' Zaccheo nodded to one of his lawyers, who passed a sheet across the desk to her father.

Eva caught a glimpse of the names on the list and flinched. While the list was only half a page, she noticed more than one global conglomerate on there.

'You'll contact the CEO of each of those companies and tell them your side of the story.'

Fear flashed across her father's face. 'What's to stop them from spilling the beans?'

Zaccheo gave that chilling half-smile. 'I have a team of lawyers who'll ensure their silence if they ever want to do business with me again.'

'You're sure they'll still want your business?' Her father's voice held a newly subdued note.

'I have it on good authority their withdrawal was merely a stance. Some to gain better leverage on certain transactions and others for appearances' sake. Once they know the truth, they'll be back on board. But even if they don't come back to GWI, the purpose of your phone call would've been achieved.'

'Is this really necessary? Your company has thrived, probably beyond your wildest dreams, even while you were locked up. And this morning's stock-market reports show your stock at an all-time high.' Eva could hear the panic in her father's voice. 'Do I really need to genuflect in front of these people to make you happy?' he added bitterly.

'Yes. You do.'

Her father's face reddened. 'Look here. Judging by that rock I see on Eva's finger, you're about to marry my daughter. We're about to be *family*. Is this really how you wish to start our familial relationship?'

Bitterness pushed aside her compassion when she realised her father was once again using her as leverage for his own ends.

'You don't think this is the least you can do, Father?' she asked.

'You're taking his side?' her father demanded.

Eva sighed. 'I'm taking the side of doing the right thing. Surely you can see that?'

Her father huffed, and Zaccheo's lips thinned into a formidable line. 'I have no interest in building a relationship with you personally. You can drop dead for all I care. Right after you carry out my instructions, of course.'

'Young man, be reasonable,' her father pleaded, realising that for once he'd come up against an immoveable object that neither his charm nor his blustering would shift.

Zaccheo stared back dispassionately. No one in the room could harbour the misguided idea that he would soften in any way.

'I don't think you have a choice in the matter, Father,' Sophie muttered into the tense silence.

Eva glanced at her sister, searching for that warmth they'd once shared. But Sophie kept her face firmly turned away.

Eva jumped as her father pushed back his chair. 'Fine, you win.'

Zaccheo brushed off imaginary lint from his sleeve. 'Excellent. And please be sure to give a convincing performance. My people will contact each CEO on that list by Friday. Make sure you get it done by then.'

Her father's barrel chest rose and fell as he tried to control his temper. 'It'll be done. Sophie, we're leaving.'

Eva started to rise, too, only to find a hand clamped on her hip. The electricity that shot through her body at the bold contact had her swaying on her feet.

'What are you doing?' she demanded.

Zaccheo ignored her, but his thumb moved lazily over her hip bone as he addressed her father. 'You and Sophie may leave. I still have things to discuss with my fiancée. My secretary will contact you with details of the wedding in the next day or two.'

Her father looked from her face to Zaccheo's. Then he stormed out of the door.

Eva turned to Zaccheo. 'What more could we possibly have to discuss? You've made everything crystal clear.'

'Not quite everything. Sit down.' He waited until she complied before he removed his hand.

Eva wasn't sure whether it was relief that burst through her chest or outrage. Relief, most definitely, she decided. Lacing her fingers, she waited as he dismissed all except one lawyer.

At Zaccheo's nod, the man produced a thick binder and placed it in front of Zaccheo, after which he also left.

She could feel Zaccheo's powerful gaze on her, but she'd already unsettled herself by looking at him once. And she was reeling from everything that had taken place here in the last hour.

When the minutes continued to tick by in silence, she raised her head. 'You want my father to help rebuild the damage he caused to your reputation, but what about your criminal record? I would've thought that would be more important to you.'

'You may marry a man with a criminal record come Saturday, but I won't remain that way for long. My lawyers are working on it.'

Her heart lurched at the reminder that in a few short days she would be his wife, but she forced herself to ask the question on her mind. 'How can they do that without implicating my father? Isn't withholding evidence a crime?'

'Nothing will be withheld. How the authorities choose to apply the rule of law is up to them.'

Recalling the state of her father's health, she tightened

her fists in anxiety. 'So you're saying Father can still go to prison? Despite letting him believe he won't?'

The kick in his stare struck deep in her soul. 'I'm the one who was wronged. I have some leeway in speaking on his behalf, should I choose to.'

The implied threat didn't escape her notice. They would either toe his line or suffer the consequences.

She swallowed. 'What did you want to discuss with me?'

He placed a single sheet of paper in front of her.

'These are the engagements we'll be attending this week. Make sure you put them in your diary.'

She pursed her lips, denying that the deep pang in her chest was hurt. 'At least you're laying your cards on the table this time round.'

'What cards would those be?'

She shrugged. 'The ones that state your desire to conquer the upper class, of course. Wasn't that your aim all along? To walk in the hallowed halls of the Old Boys' Club and show them all your contempt for them?'

His eyes narrowed, but she caught a shadow in the grey depths. 'How well you think you know me.'

She cautioned herself against probing the sleeping lion, but found herself asking anyway, 'Why, Zaccheo? Why is it so important that you bring us all down a peg or two?'

He shifted in his seat. If she hadn't known that he didn't possess an ounce of humility, she'd have thought he was uneasy. 'I don't detest the whole echelon. Just those who think they have a right to lord it over others simply because of their pedigree. And, of course, those who think they can get around the laws that ordinary people have to live by.'

'What about me? Surely you can't hate me simply because our relationship didn't work out?'

'Was that what we had—a *relationship*?' he sneered. 'I thought it was a means for you to facilitate your father's plans.'

'*What?* You think I had something to do with my father scapegoating you?'

'Perhaps you weren't privy to his whole plan like your sister was. But the timing of it all was a little too convenient, don't you think? You walked away *three days* before I was charged, with a flimsy excuse after an even flimsier row. What was it? Oh, yes, you didn't want to marry *a man like me?*'

She surged to her feet, her insides going cold. 'You think I staged the whole thing? Need I remind you that you were the one who initiated our first meeting? That you were the one to ask me out?'

'An event carefully orchestrated by your father, of course. Do you know why I was at Siren that night?'

'Will you believe me if I said no?'

'I was supposed to meet your father and two of his investors there. Except none of them showed.'

She frowned. 'That's not possible. My father hates that I sing. He hates it even more that I work in a nightclub. I don't think he even knows where Siren is.'

'And yet he suggested it. Highly recommended it, in fact.'

The idea that her father had engineered their first meeting coated her mouth with bitterness. He'd used her strong loyalty to their family to manipulate her long before she'd taken a stand and moved out of Pennington Manor. But this further evidence showed a meticulousness that made her blood run cold.

'Were you even a virgin back then?' Zaccheo sliced at her.

The question brought her back to earth. 'Excuse me?'

'Or was it a ploy to sweeten the deal?'

'I didn't know you existed until you parked yourself in front of the stage that night!'

'Maybe not. But you must've known who I was soon after. Isn't that what women do these days? A quick internet search while they're putting on their make-up to go on the first date?'

Eva couldn't stop her guilty flush because it was exactly what she'd done. But not with the reprehensible intentions he'd implied. Zaccheo's all-consuming interest in her had seemed too good to be true. She'd wanted to know more about the compelling man who'd zeroed in on her with such unnerving interest.

What she'd found was a long list of conquests ranging from supermodels to famous sports stars. She'd been so intimidated, she'd carefully kept her inexperience under wraps. It was that desperately embarrassing need to prove her sophistication that had led to her boldly accepting his dare to perform oral sex on him on his thirtieth birthday. She'd been so anxious, she'd bungled it even before she'd unfastened his belt. In the face of his wry amusement, she'd blurted her inexperience.

The inexperience he was now denouncing as a ploy.

'I don't care what you think. All I care about is that I know what I'm letting myself in for now. I know exactly the type of man you are.' One whose ruthless ambition was all he cared about.

He regarded her for several tense seconds. 'Then this won't surprise you too much.' He slid a thick burgundy folder across to her. 'It's a prenuptial agreement. On the first page you'll find a list of independent lawyers who can guide you through the legalese should you require it. The terms are non-negotiable. You have twenty-four hours to read and sign it.'

She glanced from him to the folder, her mouth dropping open in shock. 'Why would I need a prenup? I've agreed to your demands. Isn't this overkill?'

'My lawyers go spare if I don't get everything in writing. Besides, there are a few items in there we haven't discussed yet.'

Something in his voice made her skin prickle. Her belly quaked as she turned the first page of the thick document. The first few clauses were about general schedules and routines, making herself available for his engagements within reason, how many homes he owned and her duty to oversee the running of them, and his expectation of her availability to travel with him on his business trips should he require it.

'If you think I'm going to turn myself into a pet you can pick up and hop on a plane with whenever it suits you, you're in for a shock.'

He merely quirked an eyebrow at her. She bristled but carried on reading.

She paused at the sixth clause. 'We can't be apart for more than five days in the first year of marriage?'

The half-smile twitched. 'We don't want tongues wagging too soon, do we?'

'You mean after the first year I can lock myself in a nunnery for a year if I choose to?'

For the first time since Zaccheo had exploded back into her life, she glimpsed a genuine smile. It was gone before it registered fully, but the effect was no less earth-shattering. 'No nunnery would accept you once you've spent a year in my bed.'

Her face flamed and the look in his eyes made her hurriedly turn the page.

The ninth made her almost swallow her tongue. 'I don't want your money! And I certainly don't need that much money *every* month.' The sum stated was more than she earned in a year.

He shrugged. 'Then donate it to your favourite charity.'

Since she wasn't going to win that one, she moved on to the tenth and last clause.

Eva jerked to her feet, her heart pounding as she reread the words, hoping against hope that she'd got it wrong the first time. But the words remained clear and stark and *frightening*. 'You want...*children*?' she rasped through a throat gone bone dry with dread.

'*Sì,*' he replied softly. 'Two. An heir and a spare, I believe you disparagingly refer to that number in your circles. More if we're lucky—stop shaking your head, Eva.'

Eva realised that was exactly what she was doing as he rose and stalked her. She took a step back, then another, until her backside bumped the sleek black cabinet running the length of the central wall.

He stopped in front of her, leaned his tall, imposing frame over hers. 'Of all the clauses in the agreement, this is non-negotiable.'

'You said they were all non-negotiable.'

'They are, but some are more non-negotiable than others.'

A silent scream built inside her. 'If this one is the most important why did you put it last?'

'Because you would be signing directly below it. I wanted you to feel its import so there would be no doubt in your mind what you were agreeing to.'

She started to shake her head again but froze when he angled himself even closer, until their lips were an inch apart. Their breaths mingling, he stared her down. Eva's heart climbed into her throat as she struggled to sift through the emotions those words on the page had evoked.

Zaccheo was asking the impossible.

Children were the reasons why her last two relationships before him had failed before they'd even begun.

Children were the reason she'd painfully resigned herself to remaining single. To spurning any interest that came her way because she hadn't been able to bear the thought of baring her soul again only to have her emotions trampled on.

She wouldn't cry. She wouldn't break down in front of Zaccheo. Not today. *Not ever.* He'd caused her enough turmoil to last a lifetime.

But he was asking the impossible. 'I can't.'

His face hardened but he didn't move a muscle. 'You can. You *will*. Three days ago you were agreeing to marry another man. You expect me to believe the possibility of children weren't on the cards with Fairfield?'

She shook her head. 'My agreement with Harry was different. Besides, he...' She stopped, unwilling to add to the flammable tension.

'He what?' Zaccheo enquired silkily.

'He didn't *hate* me!'

He seemed almost surprised at her accusation. Surprise slowly gave way to a frown. 'I don't hate you, Eva. In fact, given time and a little work, we might even find common ground.'

She cursed her heart for leaping at his words. 'I can't—'

'You have twenty-four hours. I suggest you take the time and review your answer before saying another word.'

Her stomach clenched. 'And if my answer remains the same?'

His expression was one of pure, insufferable arrogance. 'It won't. You make feeble attempts to kick at the demands of your ancestry and title, but inevitably you choose blood over freedom. You'll do anything to save your precious family name—'

'You really think so? After the meeting we just had? Are you really that blind, or did you not see the way my sister and my father treat me? We are not a close family, Zaccheo. No matter how much I wish it...' Her voice shook, but she firmed it. 'Have you stopped to think that you pushing me this way may be the catalyst I need to completely break away from a family that's already broken?'

Her terse words made his eyes narrow. But his expression cleared almost immediately. 'No, you're loyal. You'll give me what I want.'

'No—'

'Yes,' he breathed.

He closed the gap between them slowly, as if taunting her with the knowledge that she couldn't escape the inevitability of his possession.

His mouth claimed hers—hot, demanding, powerfully erotic. Eva moaned as her emotions went into free fall. He feasted on her as if he had all the time in the world, taking turns licking his way into her mouth before sliding his tongue against hers in an expert dance that had her desperately clutching his waist.

Wild, decadent heat swirled through her body as he lifted her onto the cabinet, tugged up the hem of her dress and planted himself between her thighs. Her shoulders met the wall and she gasped as one hand gripped her thigh.

Push him away. You need to push him away!

Her hands climbed from his waist to his chest, albeit far slower and in a far more exploratory fashion than her screeching brain was comfortable with. But she made an effort once she reached his broad shoulders.

She pushed.

And found her hands captured in a firm one-handed hold above her head. His other hand found her breast and palmed it, squeezing before flicking his thumb over her hardened nipple.

Sensation pounded through her blood. Her legs curled around his thickly muscled thighs and she found herself pulled closer to the edge of the cabinet, until the powerful evidence of his erection pushed at her core.

Zaccheo gave a deep groan and freed her hands to bury his in her hair. Angling her head for a deeper invasion, he devoured her until the need for air drove them apart.

Chests heaving, they stared at each other for several seconds before Eva scrambled to untangle her legs from around him. Every skin cell on fire, she struggled to stand up. He stopped her with a hand on her belly, his eyes compelling hers so effortlessly, she couldn't look away.

The other hand moved to her cheek, then his fingers drifted over her throbbing mouth.

'As much as I'd like to take you right here on my boardroom cabinet, I have a dozen meetings to chair. It seems everyone wants a powwow with the newly emancipated CEO. We'll pick this up again at dinner. I'll be home by seven.'

She diverted enough brainpower from the erotic images it was creating to reply. 'I won't be there. I'm working tonight.'

A tic throbbed at his temple as he straightened his tie. 'I see that I need to put aligning our schedules at the top of my agenda.'

She pushed him away and stood. 'Don't strain yourself too much on my account,' she responded waspishly. She was projecting her anger at her weakness onto him, but she couldn't help herself. She tugged her dress down, painfully aware of the sensitivity between her unsteady legs as she moved away from him and picked up her handbag and the folder containing the prenup. 'I'll see you when I see you.'

He took her hand and walked her to the door. 'I guarantee you it'll be much sooner than that.' He rode the lift down with her to the ground floor, barely acknowledging the keen interest his presence provoked.

Romeo was entering the building as they exited. The two men exchanged a short conversation in Italian before Zaccheo opened the door to the limo.

When she went to slide in, he stopped her. 'Wait.'

'What is it?' she demanded.

His lips firmed and he seemed in two minds as to his response. 'For a moment during the meeting, you took my side against your father. I'll factor that favourably into our dealings from now on.'

Eva's heart lifted for a moment, then plunged back to her toes. 'You don't get it, do you?'

He frowned. 'Get what?'

'Zaccheo, for as long as I can remember, all I've wished was for there to be *no sides*. For there not to be a *them* against *us*. Maybe that makes me a fool. Or maybe I'll need to give up that dream.'

His eyes turned a shade darker with puzzlement, then he shrugged. '*Sì, bellissima*, perhaps you might have to.'

And right in front of the early lunch crowd, Zaccheo announced his ownership of her with a long, deep kiss.

* * *

Eva could barely hear herself think above the excited buzz in Siren's VIP lounge as she cued the next song.

She was sure the unusually large Monday night crowd had nothing to with Ziggy Preston, the famous record producer who'd been coming to watch her perform on and off for the past month, and everything to do with the pictures that had appeared in the early-evening paper of her kissing Zaccheo outside his office this afternoon. Avoiding the news had been difficult, seeing as that kiss and a large-scale picture of her engagement ring had made front-page news.

One picture had held the caption *'Three Ring Circus'*— with photos of her three engagement rings and a pointed question as to her motives.

It'd been a relief to leave Zaccheo's penthouse, switch off her phone and immerse herself in work. Not least because blanking her mind stopped her from thinking about the last clause in the prenup, and the reawakened agony she'd kept buried since her doctor had delivered the harrowing news six years ago. News she'd only revealed twice, with devastating consequences.

She almost wished she could blurt it out to Zaccheo and let the revelation achieve what it had in the past—a swift about-face from keen interest to cold dismissal, with one recipient informing her, in the most callous terms, that he could never accept her as a full woman.

Pain flared wider, threatening the foundations she'd built to protect herself from that stark truth. Foundations Zaccheo threatened.

She clutched the mic and forced back the black chasm that swirled with desolation. Her accompanying pianist nodded and she cleared her throat, ready to sing the ballad that ironically exhorted her to be brave.

She was halfway through the song when he walked in. As usual, the sight of him sent a tidal wave of awareness through her body and she managed to stop herself from stumbling by the skin of her teeth. Heads turned and the buzz in the room grew louder.

Zaccheo's eyes raked her from head to toe before settling on her face. A table miraculously emptied in front of the stage. Someone took his overcoat and Eva watched him release the single button to his dinner jacket before pulling out a chair and seating himself at the roped-off table before her.

The sense of déjà vu was so overwhelming, she wanted to abandon the song and flee from the stage. She finished, she smiled and accepted the applause, then made her way to where he pointedly held out a chair for her.

'What are you doing here?' she whispered fiercely.

He took his time to answer, choosing instead to pull her close and place a kiss on each cheek before drawing back to stare at her.

'You couldn't make dinner, so I brought dinner to you.'

'You really shouldn't have,' she replied, fighting the urge to rub her cheeks where his lips had been. 'Besides, I can't. My break is only twenty minutes.'

'Tonight your break is an hour, as it will be every night I choose to dine with you here instead of at our home. Now sit down and smile, *mio piccolo uccello che canta*, and pretend to our avid audience that you're ecstatically happy to see your fiancé,' he said with a tone edged in steel.

CHAPTER NINE

ZACCHEO WATCHED MYRIAD expressions chase across her face. Rebellion. Irritation. Sexual awareness. A touch of embarrassment when someone shouted their appreciation of her singing from across the room. One glance from Zaccheo silenced that inebriated guest.

But it was the shadows that lurked in her eyes that made his jaw clench. All day, through the heady challenge of getting back into the swing of business life, that look in her eyes when she'd seen his last clause in the prenuptial agreement had played on his mind. Not enough to disrupt his day, but enough for him to keep replaying the scene. Her reaction had been extreme and almost...distressed.

Yes, it bothered him that she saw making a family with him abhorrent, even though he'd known going in that, had she been given a choice, Eva would've chosen someone else, someone more *worthy* to father her children. Nevertheless, her reaction had struck hard in a place he'd thought was no longer capable of feeling hurt.

The feeling had festered, like a burr under his skin, eating away at him as the day had progressed. Until he'd abruptly ended a videoconference and walked out of his office.

He'd intended to return home and help himself to fine whisky in a toast to striking the first blow in ending Oscar Pennington's existence. Instead he'd found himself swapping his business suit for a dinner jacket and striding back out of his penthouse.

The woman who'd occupied far too much of his thoughts today swayed to her seat and sat down. The pounding in his blood that had never quite subsided after that kiss in his boardroom, and increased the moment he'd entered the

VIP room and heard her singing, accelerated when his gaze dropped to her scarlet-painted lips.

Before he'd met Eva Pennington, Zaccheo had never labelled himself a possessive guy. Although he enjoyed the thrill of the chase and inevitable capture, he'd been equally thrilled to see the back of the women he'd dated, especially when the clinginess had begun.

With Eva, he'd experienced an unprecedented and very caveman-like urge to claim her, to make sure every man within striking distance knew she belonged to him. And only him. That feeling was as unsettling as it was hard to eradicate. It wasn't helped when she toyed with her champagne glass and avoided eye contact.

'I don't appreciate you messing with my schedule behind my back, Zaccheo,' she said.

He wasn't sure why the sound of his name on her lips further spiked his libido, but he wanted to hear it again. He wanted to hear it fall from her lips in the throes of passion, as he took her to the heights of ecstasy.

Dio, he was losing it. Losing sight of his objective. Which was to make sure she understood that he intended to give no quarter in making her his.

He took a bracing sip of champagne and nodded to the hovering waiters ready to serve the meal he'd ordered.

'It was dinner here or summoning you back to the penthouse. You should be thanking me for bending like this.'

She glared. 'You really are a great loss to the Dark Ages, you know that?'

'In time you'll learn that I always get my way, Eva. *Always.*'

Her eyes met his and that intense, inexplicable connection that had throbbed between them right from the very start pulled, tightened.

'Did it even occur to you that I may have said yes if you'd asked me to have dinner with you?'

Surprise flared through him, and he found himself asking, 'Would you?'

She shrugged. 'I guess you'll never know. We need to discuss the prenup,' she said.

He knew instinctively that she was about to refuse him again. A different sort of heat bloomed in his chest. 'This isn't the time or place.'

'I don't...' She paused when the waiters arrived at the table with their first course. As if recalling where they were, she glanced round, took a deep breath, and leaned forward. 'I won't sign it.'

Won't, not *can't*, as she'd said before.

Bitterness surged through his veins. 'Because the thought of my seed growing inside you fills you with horror?'

Her fingers convulsed around her knife, but, true to her breeding, she directed it to her plate with understated elegance to cut her steak.

'Why would you want me as the mother of your children, anyway? I would've thought you'd want to spare yourself such a vivid reminder of what you've been through.'

'Perhaps I'm the one to give the Pennington name the integrity it's been so sorely lacking thus far.'

She paled, and he cursed himself for pursuing a subject that was better off discussed in private. Although he'd made sure their table was roped off and their conversation couldn't be overheard, there was still more than enough interest in them for each expression flitting across Eva's face to be captured and assessed.

'So we're your personal crusade?' she asked, a brittle smile appearing on her face as she acknowledged someone over his shoulder.

'Let's call it more of an experiment.'

Her colour rose with the passionate fury that intrigued him. 'You'd father children based on an *experiment*? After what you've been through...what we've both been through, you think that's fair to the children you intend to have to be used solely as a means for you to prove a point?' Her voice was ragged and he tensed.

'Eva—'

'No, I won't be a part of it!' Her whisper was fierce. 'My mother may have loved me in her own way, but I was still the tool she used against my father when it suited her. If my grades happened to be better than Sophie's, she would imply my father was lacking in some way. And believe me, my father didn't pull his punches when the situation was reversed.' She swallowed and raised bruised eyes to his. 'Even if I cou—wanted to why would I knowingly subject another child to what I went through? Why would I give you a child simply to use to *prove a point*?'

'You mistake my meaning. I don't intend to fail my children or use them as pawns. I intend to be there for them through thick and thin, unlike my parents were for me.' He stopped when her eyes widened. 'Does that surprise you?'

'I… Yes.'

He shrugged, even though it occurred to him that he'd let his guard down more with her than he ever had with anyone. But she had no power to hurt him. She'd already rejected him once. This time he knew the lay of the land going in. So it didn't matter if she knew his parental ambitions for the children they'd have.

'My children will be my priority, although I'll be interested to see how your family fares with being shown that things can be done differently. The *right* way.'

He watched her digest his response, watched the shadows he was beginning to detest mount in her eyes. He decided against probing further. There'd been enough turbulent emotions today. He suspected there would be further fireworks when she found out the new business negotiations he'd commenced this afternoon.

That a part of him was looking forward to it made him shift in his seat.

Since when had he craved verbal conflict with a woman?

Never. And yet he couldn't seem to help himself when it came to Eva.

He was debating this turn of events as their plates were removed when a throat cleared next to them.

The man was around his age, with floppy brown hair and a cocky smile that immediately rubbed Zaccheo the wrong way.

'Can I join you for a few minutes?' he asked.

The *no* that growled up Zaccheo's chest never made it. Eva was smiling—her first genuine smile since he'd walked in—and nodding. 'Mr Preston, of course!'

'Thanks. And call me Ziggy, please. Mr Preston is my headmaster grandfather.'

'What can we do for you, *Ziggy*?' Zaccheo raised an eyebrow at the furious look Eva shot him.

The other man, who was staring at Eva with an avidness that made Zaccheo's fist clench, finally looked in his direction. 'I came to pay my compliments to your girlfriend. She has an amazing voice.'

Eva blushed at his words.

Zaccheo's eyes narrowed when he noticed she wasn't wearing her engagement ring. 'Eva's my fiancée, not my girlfriend. And I'm very much aware of her exceptional talent,' he said, the harsh edge to his voice getting through to the man, who looked from him to Eva before his smile dimmed.

'Ah, congratulations are in order, then?'

'*Grazie,*' Zaccheo replied. 'Was there something else you wanted?'

'Zaccheo!' Eva glared harder, and turned to Ziggy. 'Pardon my *fiancé*. He's feeling a little testy because—'

'I want her all to myself but find other *things* standing in my way. And because you're not wearing your engagement ring, *dolcezza.*'

She covered her bare fingers with her hand, as if that would remove the evidence of the absence of his ring. 'Oh,

I didn't want to risk losing it. I'm still getting used to it.' The glance she sent him held a mixture of defiance and entreaty.

Ziggy cleared his throat again. 'I don't want to play the *Do-you-know-who-I-am?* card, but—'

'Of course I know who you are,' Eva replied with a charming laugh.

Ziggy smiled and produced a business card. 'In that case, would you like to come to my studio next week? See if we can make music together?'

Eva's pleased gasp further darkened Zaccheo's mood. 'Of course I can—'

'Aren't you forgetting something, *luce mio*?' he asked in a quietly lethal tone.

'What?' she asked, so innocently he wanted to grab her from the chair, spread her across the table and make her see nothing, no one, but him. Make her recall that she had given her word to be his and only his.

'You won't be available next week.' He didn't care that he hadn't yet apprised her of the details. He cared that she was smiling at another man as if *he* didn't exist. 'We'll be on our honeymoon on my private island off the coast of Brazil where we'll be staying for the next two weeks.'

Her eyes rounded, but she recovered quickly and took the business card. 'I'll *make* time to see you before I go. Surely you don't want to deny me this opportunity, *darling*?' Her gaze swung to him, daring him to respond in the negative.

Despite his irritation, Zaccheo curbed a smile. 'Of course. Anything for you, *dolcezza*.'

Ziggy beamed. 'Great! I look forward to it.'

The moment he was out of earshot, she turned to Zaccheo. 'How dare you try and sabotage me like that?'

'Watching you smile at another man like that fills me with insane jealousy. It also brings out the jerk in me. My apologies,' he growled. Her mouth dropped open. 'Close your mouth, Eva.'

She shook her head as if reeling from a body blow.

Welcome to my world.

'Where's your ring?' He stared at her, his control on a knife-edge.

Perhaps sensing the dangerously shifting currents, she pulled up the gold chain that hung between her pert, full breasts. His ring dangled from it.

'Put it on. Now,' he said, struggling to keep his voice even.

Undoing the clasp, she took the ring off the chain and slid it back on her finger. 'There. Can I return to work now or are you going to harangue me about something else?'

He told himself he did it because he needed to put his rampaging emotions *somewhere*. That it was her fault for pushing him to his limit. But when he plucked her from her seat, placed her in his lap and kissed her insanely tempting mouth, Zaccheo knew it was because he couldn't help himself. She *got* to him in a way no one else did.

By the time he pulled away, they were both breathing hard. Her high colour filled him with immense satisfaction, helping him ignore his own hopeless loss of control.

'Don't take the ring off again, Eva. You underestimate the lengths I'm prepared to go to in making sure you stick to your word, but for your sake I hope you start taking me seriously.'

In contrast to the vividness of Zaccheo's presence, the rest of the night passed in a dull blur after he left. By the time Eva collapsed into bed in the early hours, her head throbbed with the need to do something severely uncharacteristic. Like scream. Beat her fists against the nearest wall. Shout her anger and confusion to the black skies above.

She did nothing of the sort. More than anything, she craved a little peace and quiet.

After that kiss in the club, even more eyes had followed her wherever she went. Hushed whispers had trailed her to the bathroom. By the time her shift had ended three hours later, she'd been ready to walk out and never return.

She wouldn't, of course. Working at Siren gave her the free time to write her songs while earning enough to live on. Despite Zaccheo's heavy-handedness, she could never see a time when she'd be dependent on anyone other than herself.

'You underestimate the lengths I'm prepared to go to...'

The forceful statement had lingered long after he'd left, anchored by the heavy presence of the prenuptial agreement in her handbag.

He'd said he wouldn't negotiate. Eva didn't see that he had a choice in this matter. Refusing to marry him might well spell the end for her father, but withholding the truth and marrying him knowing she could never fulfil her part of the bargain would be much worse.

Turning in bed, she punched her pillow, dreading the long, restless night ahead. Only to wake with sunshine streaming through the window and her clock announcing it was ten o'clock.

Rushing out of bed, she showered quickly and entered the dining room just as Romeo was exiting, having finished his own breakfast. The table was set for one and Eva cursed herself for the strange dip in her belly that felt very much like disappointment.

'Good morning. Shall I get the chef to make you a cooked breakfast?' The man whose role she was beginning to suspect went deeper than a simple second-in-command asked.

'Just some toast and tea, please, thank you.'

He nodded and started to leave.

'Is Zaccheo around or has he left for the office?'

'Neither. He left this morning for Oman. An unexpected hiccup in the construction of his building there.'

Eva was unprepared for the bereft feeling that swept through her. She should be celebrating her temporary reprieve. Finding a way to see if she could work around that impossible clause. 'When will he be back?'

'In a day or two. Latest by the end of the week to be ready in time for the wedding,' Romeo said in that deep, modulated voice of his. 'This is for you.' He handed her a folded note and left.

The bold scrawl was unmistakeably Zaccheo's.

Eva,

Treat my absence as you wish, but never as an excuse to be complacent.

My PA will be in touch with details of your wedding dress fitting this morning and your amended schedule for the week.

You have my permission to miss me.

Z

Ugh! She grimaced at the arrogance oozing from the paper. Balling the note, she flung it across the table. Then quickly jumped up and retrieved it before Romeo returned. The last thing she wanted was for him to report her loss of temper to Zaccheo.

Her traitorous body had a hard enough time controlling itself when Zaccheo was around. She didn't want him to know he affected her just as badly when he was absent.

By the time breakfast was delivered, she'd regained her composure. Which was just as well, because close on the chef's heel was a tall, striking brunette dressed in a grey pencil skirt and matching jacket.

'Good morning, my name is Anyetta, Mr Giordano's PA. He said you were expecting me?'

'I was expecting a phone call, not a personal visit.'

Anyetta delivered a cool smile. 'Mr Giordano wanted his wishes attended to personally.'

Eva's appetite fled. 'I bet he did,' she muttered.

She poured herself a cup of tea as Anyetta proceeded to fill up her every spare hour between now and Saturday morning.

Eva listened until her temper began to flare, then tuned

out until she heard the word *makeover*. 'I've already had one makeover. I don't need another one.'

Anyetta's eyes drifted over Eva's hair, which she admitted was a little wild since she hadn't brushed it properly before she'd rushed out to speak to Zaccheo. 'Not even for your wedding day?'

Since there wasn't likely to be a wedding day once she told Zaccheo she had no intention of signing the agreement, she replied, 'It'll be taken care of.'

Anyetta ticked off a few more items, verified that Eva's passport was up to date, then stood as the doorbell rang. 'That'll be Margaret with your wedding dress.'

The feeling of being on a runaway train intensified as Eva trailed Anyetta out of the dining room. She drew to a stunned halt when she saw the middle-aged woman coming towards her with a single garment bag and a round veil and shoebox.

'Please tell me you don't have a team of assistants lurking outside ready to jump on me?' she asked after Anyetta left.

Margaret laughed. 'It's just me, Lady Pennington. Your fiancé was very specific about his wishes, and, meeting you now, I see why he chose this dress. He did say I was to work with you, of course. So if you don't like it, we can explore other options.'

Eva reminded herself that this situation hadn't arisen out of a normal courtship, that Zaccheo choosing her wedding dress for her shouldn't upset her so much. Besides, the likelihood of this farce ever seeing the light of day was very low so she was better off just going along with it.

But despite telling herself not to care, Eva couldn't suppress her anxiety and excitement.

She gasped as the dress was revealed.

The design itself was simple and clean, but utterly breathtaking. Eva stared at the fitted white satin gown overlaid with lace and beaded with countless tiny crystals. Delicate capped sleeves extended from the sweetheart neckline and the tiniest train flared out in a beautiful arc. At the back, more crystals had been embedded in mother-of-pearl buttons that went from nape to waist. Unable to resist, Eva reached out to touch the dress, then pulled herself back.

There was no point falling in love with a dress she'd never wear. No point getting butterflies about a marriage that would never happen once she confessed her flaw to Zaccheo. Her hands fisted and she fought the desolation threatening to break free inside her.

For six years, she'd successfully not dwelt on what she could never have—a husband who cared for her and a family of her own. She'd made music her life and had found fulfilment in it. She wasn't about to let a heartbreakingly gorgeous dress dredge up agonies she'd sealed in a box marked *strictly out of bounds*.

'Are you ready to try it on?' Margaret asked.

Eva swallowed. 'Might as well.'

If the other woman found her response curious, she didn't let on. Eva avoided her gaze in the mirror as the dress was slipped over her shoulders and the delicate chiffon and lace veil was fitted into place. She mumbled her thanks as Margaret helped her into matching-coloured heels.

'Oh, I'm pleased to see we don't need to alter it in any way, Lady Pennington. It fits perfectly. Looks like your fiancé was very accurate with your measurements. You'd be surprised how many men get it wrong…'

She kept her gaze down, frightened to look at herself, as Margaret tweaked and tugged until she was happy.

Eva dared not look up in case she began to *hope* and *wish*. She murmured appropriate responses and turned this way and that when asked and breathed a sigh of relief when the ordeal was over. The moment Margaret zipped up the bag and left, Eva escaped to her suite. Putting her headphones on, she activated the music app on her tablet and proceeded to drown out her thoughts the best way she knew how.

But this time no amount of doing what she loved best could obliterate the thoughts tumbling through her head.

At seventeen when her periods had got heavier and more painful with each passing month, she'd attributed it to life's natural cycle. But when stronger painkillers had barely alleviated the pain, she'd begun to suspect something major was wrong.

Collapsing during a university lecture had finally prompted her to seek medical intervention.

The doctor's diagnosis had left her reeling.

Even then, she'd convinced herself it wasn't the end of the world, that compared to her mother's fight against cancer, a fight she'd eventually lost a year later, Eva's problem was inconsequential. Women dealt with challenging problems like hers every day. When the time came, the man she chose to spend the rest of her life with would understand and support her.

Eva scoffed at her naiveté. Scott, the first man she'd dated in the last year of university, had visibly recoiled from her when she'd mentioned her condition. She'd been so shocked by his reaction, she'd avoided him for the rest of her time at uni.

Burnt, she'd sworn off dating until she'd met George Tremayne, her fellow business intern during her brief stint at Penningtons. Flattered by his attentiveness, she'd let down her guard and gone on a few dates before he'd begun to pressure her to take things further. Her gentle rejection and confession of her condition had resulted in a scathing volley of insults, during which she'd found out exactly why her father had been pressing her to work at Penningtons after graduation.

Oscar Pennington, already secure in his conscript of Sophie as his heir, was eager to offload his remaining daughter and had lined up a list of suitable men, George Tremayne, the son of a viscount, being on the top of that list. George's near-identical reaction to Scott's had hurt twice as much, and convinced Eva once and for all that her secret was best kept to herself.

Finding out she was yet another means to an end for Zaccheo had rocked her to the core, but she'd taken consolation in the fact the secret she'd planned on revealing to him shortly after their engagement was safe.

That secret was about to be ripped open.

As she turned up the volume of her music Eva knew disclosing it to Zaccheo would be the most difficult thing she would ever do.

CHAPTER TEN

ZACCHEO SCROLLED THROUGH the missed calls from Eva on his phone as he was driven away from the private hangar. Romeo had relayed her increasingly frantic requests to reach him. Zaccheo had deliberately forbidden his number from being given to her until this morning, once he'd confirmed his return to London.

His jaw flexed as he rolled tight shoulders. The number of fires he'd put out in Oman would've wiped out a lesser man. But Zaccheo's name and ruthless nature weren't renowned for nothing, and although it'd taken three days to get the construction schedule back on track, his business partners were in no doubt that he would bring them to their knees if they strayed so much as one millimetre from the outcome he desired.

It was the same warning he'd given Oscar Pennington when he'd called yesterday and attempted an ego-stroking exercise to get Zaccheo to relent on his threats. Zaccheo had coldly reminded him of the days he'd spent in prison and invited Pennington to ask for clemency when hell froze over.

No doubt Eva's eagerness to contact him was born of the same desire as her father's. But unlike her father, the thought of speaking to Eva sent a pleasurable kick of anticipation through his blood, despite the fact that with time and distance he'd looked back on their conversations since his release with something close to dismay.

Had he really revealed all those things about his time in prison and his childhood to her?

What was even more puzzling was her reaction. She hadn't looked down her nose at him in those moments. Had in fact exhibited nothing but empathy and compassion. Pushing the bewildering thought away, he dialled her number, gratified when she picked up on the first ring.

'*Ciao*, Eva. I understand you're experiencing pre-wedding jitters.'

'You understand wrong. This wedding isn't going to happen. Not once you hear what I have to say.'

His tension increased until the knots in his shoulders felt like immoveable rocks. He breathed through the red haze blurring his vision. 'I take it you didn't miss me, then?' he taunted.

She made a sound, a cross between a huff and a sigh. 'We really need to talk, Zaccheo.'

'Nothing you say will alter my intention to make you mine tomorrow,' he warned.

She hesitated. Then, 'Zaccheo, it's important. I won't take up too much of your time. But I need to speak to you.'

He rested his head against the seat. 'You have less than twenty-four hours left as a single woman. I won't permit anything like male strippers anywhere near you, of course, but I won't be a total bore and deny you a hen party if you wish—'

'I don't want a damn hen party! What I want is five minutes of your time.'

'Are you dying of some life-threatening disease?'

'*What?* Of course not!'

'Are you afraid I won't be a good husband?' he asked, noting the raw edge to his voice, but realising how much her answer meant to him.

'Zaccheo, this is about me, not you.'

He let her non-answer slide. 'You'll be a good wife. And despite your less than auspicious upbringing, you'll be a good mother.'

He heard her soft gasp. 'How do you know that?'

'Because you're passionate when you care. You just need to channel that passion from your undeserving family to the one we will create.'

'I can't just switch my feelings towards my family off.

Everyone deserves someone who cares about them, no matter what.'

His heart kicked hard and his grip tightened around the phone as bitterness washed through him. 'Not everyone gets it, though.'

Silence thrummed. 'I'm sorry about your parents. Is... your mother still alive?' Her voice bled the compassion he'd begun to associate with her.

It warmed a place inside him even as he answered. 'That depends on who you ask. Since she relocated to the other side of the world to get away from me, I presume she won't mind if I think her dead to me.'

'But she's alive, Zaccheo. Which means there's hope. Do you really want to waste that?' Her pain-filled voice drew him up short, reminding him that she'd lost her mother.

When had this conversation turned messy and emotional?

'You were close to your mother?' he asked.

'When she wasn't busy playing up to being a Pennington, or using me to get back at my father, she was a brilliant mother. I wish... I wish she'd been a mother to both Sophie *and* me.' She laughed without humour. 'Hell, I used to wish I'd been born into another family, that my last name wasn't Pennington—' She stopped and a tense silence reigned.

Zaccheo frowned. Things weren't adding up with Eva. He'd believed her surname was one she would do just about anything for, including help cover up fraud. But in his boardroom on Monday, she'd seemed genuinely shocked and hurt by the extent of her father's duplicity. And there was also the matter of her chosen profession and the untouched money in her bank account.

A less cynical man would believe she was the exception to the abhorrent aristocratic rule...

'At least you had one parent who cared for you. You were lucky,' he said, his mind whirling with the possibility that he could be wrong.

'But that parent is gone, and I feel as if I have no one now,' she replied quietly.

The need to tell her she had him flared through his mind. He barely managed to stay silent. After a few seconds, she cleared her throat. Her next words made him wish he'd hung up.

'I haven't signed the prenup,' she blurted out. 'I'm not going to.'

Because of the last clause.

For a brief moment, Zaccheo wanted to tell her why he wanted children. That the bleak loneliness that had dogged him through his childhood and almost drowned him in prison had nearly broken him. That he'd fallen into a pit of despair when he'd realised no one would miss him should the worst happen.

His mother had emigrated to Australia with her husband rather than stay in the same city as him once Zaccheo had fully established himself in London. That had cut deeper than any rejection he'd suffered from her in the past. And although the news of his trial and sentencing had been worldwide news, Zaccheo had never once heard from the woman who'd given him life.

He could've died in prison for all his mother cared. That thought had haunted him day and night until he'd decided to do something about it.

Until he'd vowed to alter his reality, ensure he had someone who would be proud to bear his name. Someone to whom he could pass on his legacy.

He hadn't planned for that person to be Eva Pennington until he'd read about her engagement in the file. But once he had, the decision had become iron cast.

Although this course was very much a sweeter, more lasting experience, Zaccheo couldn't help but wonder if it was all worth the ground shifting so much beneath his feet.

Eva was getting beneath his skin. And badly.

Dio mio. Why were the feelings he'd bottled up for over two decades choosing *now* to bubble up? He exhaled harshly.

Rough and ruthless was his motto. It was what had made him the man he was today. 'You'll be in your wedding dress at noon tomorrow, ready to walk down the aisle where our six hundred guests will be—'

'*Six hundred?* You've invited six *hundred* people to the wedding?' Her husky disbelief made his teeth grind.

'You thought I intended to have a hole-in-the-wall ceremony?' A fresh wave of bitterness rolled over him. 'Or did you think my PA was spouting gibberish when she informed you of all this on Tuesday?'

'Sorry, I must've tuned out because, contrary to what you think, I don't like my life arranged for me,' she retorted. 'That doesn't change anything. I *can't* do this...'

Zaccheo frowned at the naked distress in her voice.

Eva was genuinely torn up about the prospect of giving herself to him, a common man only worthy of a few kisses but nothing as substantial as the permanent state of matrimony.

Something very much like pain gripped his chest. 'Is that your final decision? Are you backing out of our agreement?'

She remained silent for so long, he thought the line was dead. 'Unless you're willing to change the last clause, yes.'

Zaccheo detested the sudden clenching of his stomach, as if the blow he'd convinced himself would never come had been landed. The voice taunting him for feeling more than a little stunned was ruthlessly smashed away.

He assured himself he had another way to claim the justice he sought. 'Very well. *Ciao.*'

He ended the phone call. And fought the urge to hurl his phone out of the window.

Eva dropped the phone onto the coffee-shop table. She'd arrived at work only to discover she'd been taken off the roster due to her impending wedding. Since she had holiday due to her anyway, Eva hadn't fought too hard at suddenly finding herself with free time.

Her session with Ziggy yesterday had gone well, despite her head being all over the place. If nothing else came of it, she could add that to her CV.

Curbing a hysterical snort, she stared at her phone.

She'd done the right thing and ended this farce before it went too far. Before the longings she'd harboured in the last three days got any more out of control.

Deep in her heart, she knew Zaccheo would react the same way to her secret as Scott and George had. He wouldn't want to marry half a woman, especially when he'd stated his expectations in black and white in a formal agreement drafted by a team of lawyers, and then confounded her with his genuine desire to become a father.

So why hadn't she just told him over the phone?

Because she was a glutton for punishment?

Because some part of her had hoped telling him face-to-face would help her gauge whether there was a chance he would accept her the way she was?

Fat chance.

It was better this way. Clean. Painless.

She jumped as her phone pinged. Heart lurching, she accessed the message, but it was only the manageress from Siren, wishing her a lovely wedding and sinfully blissful honeymoon.

Eva curled her hand around her fast-cooling mug. Once the news got out that she'd broken her third engagement in two years, her chances of marrying anyone, let alone a man who would accept her just as she was, would shrink from nil to no chance in hell.

Pain spiked again at the reminder of her condition. Exhaling, she wrenched her mind to more tangible things.

Like finding a place to live.

She weighed her options, despair clutching her insides

when, two hours later, she faced the only avenue open to her. Going back home to Pennington Manor.

Reluctantly, she picked up her phone, then nearly dropped it when it blared to life. The name of the caller made her frown.

'Sophie?'

'Eva, what's going on?' The fear in her voice shredded Eva's heart.

'What do you mean?'

'I've just had to call the doctor because Father's had another episode!'

Eva jerked to her feet, sending her coffee cup bouncing across the table. 'What?'

'We got a call from Zaccheo Giordano an hour ago to say the wedding was off. Father's been frantic. He was about to call you when he collapsed. The doctor says if he's subjected to any more stress he could have a heart attack or a stroke. Is it true? Did you call off the wedding?' The strain in her sister's voice was unmistakeable.

'Yes,' Eva replied. She grabbed her bag and hurried out of the coffee shop when she began to attract peculiar looks. Outside, she shrugged into her coat and pulled up her hoodie to avoid the light drizzle.

'Oh, God. Why?' her sister demanded.

'Zaccheo wanted me to sign a prenuptial agreement.'

'So? Everyone does that these days.'

'One of the terms…he wants *children*.'

Her sister sighed. 'So he backed out when you told him?'

'No, he doesn't know.'

'But… I'm confused,' Sophie replied.

'I tried to tell him but he wouldn't listen.'

'You tried. Isn't that enough?'

Eva ducked into a quiet alley and leaned against a wall. 'No, it's *not* enough. We've caused enough harm where he's concerned. I won't go into this based on a lie.'

'Father's terrified, Eva.'

'Can I talk to him?'

'He's sleeping now. I'll let him know you called when he wakes up.' Sophie paused. 'Eva, I've been thinking…what you said on Saturday, about you not being out to replace me… I shouldn't have bitten your head off. It's just… Father isn't an easy man to please. He was relying on me to see us through this rough patch…'

'I didn't mean to step on your toes, Sophie.'

Her sister inhaled deeply. 'I know. But everything seems so effortless for you, Eva. It always has. I envied you because Mother chose you—'

'Parents shouldn't choose which child to love and which to keep at arm's length!'

'But that was our reality. He wanted a son. And I was determined to be that son. After Mother died, I was scared Father would think I wasn't worth his attention.'

'You were. You still are.'

'Only because I've gone along with whatever he's asked of me without complaint, even when I knew I shouldn't. This thing with Zaccheo… Father's not proud of it. Nor am I. I don't know where we go from here, but once we're through this, can we get together?' Sophie asked, her voice husky with the plea.

Eva didn't realise her legs had given way until her bottom touched the cold, hard ground.

'Yes, if you want,' she murmured. Her hands shook as she hung up.

The last time she'd seen Sophie's rigid composure crumble had been in the few weeks after they'd buried their mother. For a while she'd had her sister back. They'd been united in their grief, supporting each other when their loss overwhelmed them.

As much as Eva missed *that* Sophie, she couldn't stomach having her back under similar circumstances. Nor could she bear the danger that her father faced.

She wasn't sure how long she sat there.

Cold seeped into her clothes. Into her bones. Into her heart.

Feeling numb, she dug into her bag and extracted the pre-nup and read through it one more time.

She couldn't honour Zaccheo's last clause, but that didn't mean she couldn't use it to buy herself, and her father, time until they met and she explained. Despite his own past, he wanted a family. Maybe he would understand why she was trying to salvage hers.

Slowly, she dialled. After endless rings, the line clicked through.

'Eva.' His voice was pure cold steel.

'I...' She attempted to say the words but her teeth still chattered. Squeezing her eyes shut, she tried again. 'I'll sign the agreement. I'll marry you tomorrow.'

Silence.

'Zaccheo? Are you there?'

'Where are you?'

She shivered at his impersonal tone. 'I'm...' She looked up at the street sign in the alley and told him.

'Romeo will be there in fifteen minutes. He'll witness the agreement and bring it to me. You'll return to the penthouse and resume preparations for the wedding.' He paused, as if waiting for her to disagree.

'Will I see you today?' She hated how weak her voice sounded.

'No.'

Eva exhaled. 'Okay, I'll wait for Romeo.'

'Bene.' The line went dead.

The grey mizzle outside aptly reflected Eva's mood as she sat, hands clasped in her lap, as the hairdresser finished putting up her hair. Behind her, Sophie smiled nervously.

Eva smiled back, knowing her sister's nervousness stemmed from the fear that Eva would change her mind again.

But this time there was no going back. She meant to come clean to Zaccheo at the first opportunity and open herself up to whatever consequences he sought.

Just how she would manage that was a puzzle she hadn't untangled yet, but since Zaccheo was hell-bent on this marriage, and she was giving him what he wanted, technically she was fulfilling her side of the bargain.

God, when had she resorted to seeing things in shades of grey instead of black and white, truth and lie? Was Zaccheo right? Did her Pennington blood mean she was destined to do whatever it took, even if it meant compromising her integrity, for the sake of her family and pedigree?

No. She wouldn't care if she woke up tomorrow as ordinary Eva Penn instead of Lady Pennington. And she *would* come clean to Zaccheo, no matter what.

Except that was looking less likely to happen *before* the wedding. Zaccheo hadn't returned to the penthouse last night. She hadn't deluded herself that he was observing the quaint marriage custom. If anything, he was probably making another billion, or actively sowing his last wild oats. She jerked at the jagged pain that shot through her.

Sophie stood up. 'What's wrong?'

'Nothing. How's Father?'

Sophie's face clouded. 'He insists he's well enough to walk you down the aisle.' Her sister's eyes darted to the hairdresser who had finished and was walking out to get Margaret. 'He's desperate that everything goes according to plan today.'

Eva managed to stop her smile from slipping. 'It will.'

Sophie met her gaze in the mirror. 'Do you think I should talk to Zaccheo...explain?'

Eva thought about the conversation she'd had with Zaccheo yesterday, the merciless tone, the ruthless man on a mission who'd been released from prison a mere week ago. 'Maybe not just yet.'

Sophie nodded, then flashed a smile that didn't quite make it before she left Eva alone as Margaret entered.

Any hopes of talking to Zaccheo evaporated when she found herself at the doors of the chapel an hour later.

Catching sight of him for the first time since Monday, she felt her heart slam around her chest.

Romeo stood in the best-man position and Eva wondered again at the connection between the two men. Did Zaccheo have any friends? Or had he lost all of them when her family's actions had altered his fate?

The thought flitted out of her head as her gaze returned almost magnetically to Zaccheo.

He'd eschewed a morning coat in favour of a bespoke three-piece suit in the softest dove-grey silk. Against the snowy white shirt and white tie completing the ensemble, his long hair was at once dangerously primitive and yet so utterly captivating, her mouth dried as her pulse danced with a dark, decadent delight. His beard had been trimmed considerably and a part of her mourned its loss. Perhaps it was that altered look that made his eyes so overwhelmingly electrifying, or it was the fact that his face was set in almost brutal lines, but the effect was like lightning to her system the moment her eyes connected with his.

The music in the great hall of the cathedral he'd astonishingly managed to secure on such short notice disappeared, along with the chatter of the goggle-eyed guests who did nothing to hide their avid curiosity.

All she could see was him, the man who would be her husband in less than fifteen minutes.

She stumbled, then stopped. A murmur rose in the crowd. Eva felt her father's concerned stare, but she couldn't look away from Zaccheo.

His nostrils flared, his eyes narrowing in warning as fear clutched her, freezing her feet.

'Eva?' Her father's ragged whisper caught her consciousness.

'Why did you insist on walking me down the aisle?' she asked him, wanting in some way to know that she wasn't doing all of this to save a man who had very little regard for her.

'What? Because you're my daughter,' her father replied with a puzzled frown.

'So you're not doing it just to keep up appearances?'

His face creased with a trace of the vulnerability she'd glimpsed only once before, when her mother died, and her heart lurched. 'Eva, I haven't handled things well. I know that. I was brought up to put the family name above all else, and I took that responsibility a little too far. Despite our less than perfect marriage, your mother was the one who would pull me back to my senses when I went a little too far. Without her...' His voice roughened and his hand gripped hers. 'We might lose Penningtons, but I don't want to lose you and Sophie.'

Eva's throat clogged. 'Maybe you should tell her that? She needs to know you're proud of her, Father.'

Her father looked to where her sister stood, and he nodded. 'I will. And I'm proud of you, too. You're as beautiful as your mother was on our wedding day.'

Eva blinked back her tears as murmurs rose in the crowd.

She turned to find Zaccheo staring at her. Something dark, sinister, curled through his eyes and she swallowed as his mouth flattened.

I can't marry him without him knowing! He deserves to know that I can't give him the family he wants.

'My dear, you need to move now. It's time,' her father pleaded.

Torn by the need for Zaccheo to know the truth and the need to protect her father, she shook her head, her insides churning.

Churning turned into full-blown liquefying as Zaccheo stepped from the dais, his imposing body threatening to block out the light as he headed down the aisle.

She desperately sucked in a breath, the knowledge that Zaccheo would march her up the aisle himself if need be finally scraping her feet from the floor. He stopped halfway, his gaze unswerving, until she reached him.

He grasped her hand, his hold unbreakable as he turned and walked her to the altar.

Trembling at the hard, pitiless look in his eyes, she swallowed and tried to speak. 'Zaccheo—'

'No, Eva. No more excuses,' he growled.

The priest glanced between them, his expression benign but enquiring.

Zaccheo nodded.

The organ swelled. And sealed her fate.

CHAPTER ELEVEN

'GLARING AT IT won't make it disappear, unless you have superhero laser vision.'

Eva jumped at the mocking voice and curled her fingers into her lap, hiding the exquisite diamond-studded platinum ring that had joined her engagement ring three hours ago.

'I wasn't willing it away.' On the contrary, she'd been wondering how long it would stay on her finger once Zaccheo knew the truth.

The reception following the ceremony had been brief but intense. Six hundred people clamouring for attention and the chance to gawp at the intriguing couple could take a lot out of a girl. With Zaccheo's fingers laced through hers the whole time, tightening commandingly each time she so much as moved an inch away from him, Eva had been near-blubbering-wreck status by the time their limo had left the hall.

Once she'd stopped reeling from the shock of being married to Zaccheo Giordano, she'd taken a moment to take in her surroundings. The Great Hall in the Guildhall was usually booked for years in advance. That Zaccheo had managed to secure it in a week and thrown together a stunning reception was again testament that she'd married a man with enough power and clout to smash through any resistance.

Zaccheo, despite his spell in prison, remained a formidable man, one, she suspected, who didn't need her father's intervention to restore his damaged reputation. So why was he pursuing it so relentlessly? Throughout the reception, she'd watched him charm their guests with the sheer force of his charisma. By the time her father had got round to giving the edifying toast welcoming Zaccheo to the Pennington family, the effort had seemed redundant.

She watched Zaccheo now as the car raced them to the airport, and wondered if it was a good time to broach the subject burning a hole in her chest.

'Something on your mind?' he queried without raising his gaze from his tablet.

Her heart leapt into her throat. She started to speak but noticed the partition between them and Romeo, who sat in the front passenger seat, was open. Although she was sure Romeo knew the ins and outs of the document he'd been asked to witness yesterday, Eva wasn't prepared to discuss her devastating shortcomings in his presence.

So she opted for something else plaguing her. She smoothed her hands on her wedding dress. 'Do I have your assurance that you'll speak on my father's behalf once you hand over the documents to the authorities?'

He speared her with incisive grey eyes. 'You're so eager to see him let off the hook, aren't you?'

'Wouldn't you be, if it was your father?' she asked.

Eva was unprepared for the strange look that crossed his face. The mixture of anger, sadness, and bitterness hollowed out her stomach.

'My father wasn't interested in being let off the hook for his sins. He was happy to keep himself indebted to his betters because he thought that was his destiny.'

Her breath caught. 'What? That doesn't make sense.'

'Very little of my father's actions made sense to me, not when I was a child, and not as an adult.'

The unexpected insight into his life made her probe deeper. 'When did he die?'

'When I was thirteen years old.'

'I'm sorry.' When he inclined his head and continued to stare at her, she pressed her luck. 'How did he—?'

'Zaccheo,' Romeo's deep voice interrupted them. 'Perhaps this is not a subject for your wedding day?'

A look passed between the friends.

When Zaccheo looked at her again, that cool impassivity he'd worn since they'd left the reception to thunderous applause had returned.

'Your father has done his part adequately for now. Our lawyers will meet in a few days to discuss the best way forward. When my input is needed, I'll provide it. *Your* role, on the other hand, is just beginning.'

Before she could reply, the door opened. Eva gaped at the large private jet standing mere feet away. Beside the steps, two pilots and two stewardesses waited.

Zaccheo exited and took her hand. The shocking electricity of his touch and the awareness in his eyes had her scrambling to release her fingers, but he held on, and walked her to his crew, who extended their congratulations.

Eva was grappling with their conversation when she stepped into the unspeakable luxury of the plane. To the right, a sunken entertainment area held a semicircular cream sofa and a separate set of club chairs with enough gadgets to keep even the most attention-deficient passenger happy. In a separate area a short flight of stairs away, there was a conference table with four chairs and a bar area off a top-line galley.

Zaccheo stepped behind her and her body zapped to life, thrilling to his proximity. She suppressed a shiver when he let go of her fingers and cupped her shoulders in his warm hands.

'I have several conference calls to make once we take off. And you…' He paused, traced a thumb across her cheek. The contact stunned her, as did the gentle look in his eyes. 'You look worn out.'

'Is that a kind way of saying I look like hell?' She strove for a light tone and got a husky one instead.

That half-smile appeared, and Eva experienced something close to elation that the icy look had melted from his face. 'You could never look like hell, *cara*. A prickly and challenging puzzle that I look forward to unravelling, most definitely. But never like hell.'

The unexpected response startled her into gaping for several seconds before she recovered. 'Should I be wary that you're being nice to me?'

'I can be less…monstrous when I get my way.'

The reminder that he wouldn't be getting his way and the thought of his reaction once he found out brought a spike of anxiety, rendering her silent as he led her to a seat and handed her a flute of champagne from the stewardess's tray.

'Zaccheo…' She stopped when his thumb moved over her lips. Sensation sizzled along her nerve endings, setting her pulse racing as he brushed it back and forth. The heat erupting between her thighs had her pressing her legs together to soothe the desperate ache.

She hardly felt the plane take off. All she was aware of was the mesmerising look in Zaccheo's eyes.

'I haven't told you how stunning you look.' He leaned closer and replaced his thumb with his lips at the corner of her mouth.

Delicious flames warmed her blood. 'Thank you.' Her voice shook with the desire moving through her. More than anything, she was filled with the blind need to turn her head and meet his mouth with hers.

When his lips trailed to her jaw, then to the curve between her shoulder and neck, Eva let out a helpless moan, her heart racing with sudden, debilitating hunger.

His fingers linked hers and she found herself being led to the back of the plane. Eva couldn't summon a protest. Nor could she remind herself that she needed to come clean, sooner rather than later.

The master bedroom was equally stunning. Gold leaf threaded a thick cream coverlet on a king-sized bed and plush carpeting absorbed their footsteps as he shut the door.

'I intend us to have two uninterrupted weeks on the island. In order for that to happen, I need to work with Romeo to clear my plate work-wise. Rest now. Whatever's on your mind can wait for a few more hours.' Again there was no bite to his words, leaving her lost as to this new side of the man she'd married.

She stood, almost overpowered by the strength of her emotions, as he positioned himself behind her and slowly undid her buttons. The heavy dress pooled at her feet and she stood in only her white strapless bra, panties, and the garter and sheer stocking set that had accompanied her dress.

A rough, tortured sound echoed around the room. *'Stai mozzafiato,'* Zaccheo muttered thickly. 'You're breathtaking,' he translated when she glanced at him.

A fierce blush flared up. Eyes darkening, he circled her, tracing her high colour with a barest tip of his forefinger. Her gaze dropped to the sensual line of his mouth and she bit her own lip as need drowned her.

She gasped, completely enthralled, as he dropped to his knees and reached for her garter belt, eyes locked on hers. He pulled it off and tucked it deep in his inner pocket. When he stood, the hunger on his face stopped her breath, anticipation sparking like fireworks through her veins.

He lightly brushed her lips with his.

'Our first time won't be on a plane within listening distance of my staff.' He walked to the bed and pulled back the covers. He waited until she got in and tucked her in. About to walk away, he suddenly stopped. 'We will make this marriage work, Eva.'

Her mouth parted but, with no words to counter that unexpected vow, she slowly pressed her lips together as pain ripped through her.

'Sleep well, *dolcezza*,' he murmured, then left.

Despite her turmoil, she slept through the whole flight, rousing refreshed if unsettled as to what the future held.

Dressing in a light cotton sundress and open sandals, she left her hair loose, applied a touch of lip gloss and sunscreen and exited the plane.

They transferred from jet to high-speed boat with Romeo at the wheel. The noise from the engine made conversation impossible but, for the first time, the silence between Zaccheo and Eva felt less fraught. The strange but intense feeling that had engulfed them both as he'd undressed her on the plane continued to grip them as they raced towards their final destination. When she caught her hair for the umpteenth time to keep it from flying in the wind, he captured the strands in a tight grip at the base of her neck, then used the hold to pull her closer until she curved into his side. With his other arm sprawled along the back of their seat, he appeared the most at ease Eva had ever seen him.

Perhaps being forced to wait for a while to tell him hadn't been a bad thing.

She let the tension ooze out of her.

Despite the shades covering his eyes, he must have sensed her scrutiny, because he turned and stared down at her for endless minutes. She felt the power of that look to the tips of her toes and almost fell into him when he took her mouth in a voracious kiss.

He let her up for air when her lungs threatened to burst. Burying his face in her throat, he rasped for her ears only, 'I cannot wait to make you mine.'

By the time the boat slowed and pulled into a quiet inlet, Eva was a nervous wreck.

'Welcome to Casa do Paraíso,' he said once the engine died.

Enthralled, Eva looked around. Tropical trees and lush vegetation surrounded a spectacular hacienda made of timber and glass, the mid-morning sun casting vibrant shades of green, orange and blue on the breathtaking surroundings. Wide glass windows dominated the structure and, through them, Eva saw white walls and white furniture with splashes of colourful paintings on the walls perpetuated in an endless flow of rooms.

'It's huge,' she blurted.

Zaccheo jumped onto the sugary sand and grabbed her hand.

'The previous owner built it for his first wife and their eight children. She got it in the divorce, but hated the tropical heat so never visited. It was run-down by the time I bought the island from her, so I made substantial alterations.'

The mention of children ramped up the tension crawling through her belly and, despite her trying to shrug the feeling away, it lingered as she followed him up the wide front porch into the stunning living room.

A staff of four greeted them, then hurried out to where Romeo was securing the vessel. She gazed around in stunned awe, accepting that Zaccheo commanded the best when it came to the structures he put his stamp on, whether commercial or private.

'Come here, Eva.' The order was impatient.

She turned from admiring the structure to admire the man who'd created it. Tall, proud and intensely captivating, he stood at the base of a suspended staircase, his white-hot gaze gleaming dangerously, promising complete sexual oblivion.

Desire pulsed between them, a living thing that writhed, consumed with a hunger that demanded to be met, fulfilled.

Eva knew she should make time now they were here to tell him. Lay down the truth ticking away inside her like a bomb.

After years of struggling to forge a relationship with her father and sister, she'd finally laid the foundations of one today.

How could she live with herself if she continued to keep Zaccheo in the dark about the family he hoped for himself?

Her feet slapped against the large square tiles as she hurried across the room. His mouth lifted in a half-smile of satisfaction. She'd barely reached him when he swung her into his arms and stormed up the stairs.

And then the need to disclose her secret was suddenly no longer urgent. It'd been superseded by another, more pressing demand. One that every atom in her body urged her to assuage. *Now.* Before the opportunity was taken from her. Before her confession once again found her in the brutal wasteland of rejection.

His heat singed where they touched. Unable to resist, she sank her fingers into his hair and buried her face in his neck, eager to be closer to his rough primitiveness.

Feeling bold, she nipped at his skin.

His responding growl was intoxicating. As was the feeling of being pressed against the hard, masculine planes of his body when he slowly lowered her to her feet.

'I've waited so long to be inside you. I won't wait any longer,' he vowed, the words fierce, stamped with decadent intent.

Arms clamped around her waist, he walked her backwards to the vast white-sheeted bed. In one clean move, he pulled her dress over her head and dropped it. Her bra and panties swiftly followed.

Zaccheo stopped breathing as he stared down at her exposed curves.

As he'd done on the plane, he circled her body, this time trailing more fingers over her heated skin, creating a fiery path that arrowed straight between her thighs. She was swaying under the dizzying force of her arousal by the time he faced her again.

'Beautiful. So beautiful,' he murmured against her skin, then pulled her nipple into his mouth, surrounding the aching bud with heat and want.

Eva cried out and clutched his shoulders, her whole body gripped with a fever that shook her from head to toe. He moved his attention to her twin breast while his fingers teased the other, doubling the pleasure, doubling her agony.

'Zaccheo,' she groaned.

He straightened abruptly and reefed his black T-shirt over his head, exposing hard, smooth pecs and a muscle-ridged stomach. But as intensely delectable as his torso was, it wasn't what made her belly quiver. It was the intriguing tattooed band of Celtic knots linked by three slim lines that circled his upper arm. The artwork was flawless and beautiful, flowing gracefully when he moved. Reaching out, she touched the first knot. He paused and stared down at her.

It struck her hard in that moment just how much she didn't know about the man she'd married.

'You seem almost nervous, *dolcezza.*'

Eva struggled to think of a response that wouldn't make her sound gauche. 'Don't you feel nervous, even a little, your first time with a new lover?' she replied.

He froze and his lips compressed for a fraction of a second, as if she'd said something to displease him. Then his fingers went to his belt. 'Nerves, no. Anticipation that a long-held desire is about to be fulfilled? Most definitely.' He removed his remaining clothes in one swift move.

Perfection. It was the only word she could think of.

'Even when you've experienced it more than a few dozen times?'

She gasped when his fingers gripped hers in a tight hold. When he spoke, his voice held a bite that jarred. 'Perhaps we should refrain from the subject of past lovers.'

Hard, demanding lips slanted over hers, his tongue sliding into her mouth, fracturing the last of her senses. She clung to him, her body once again aflame from the ferocious power of his.

Cool sheets met her back and Zaccheo sprawled beside her. After an eternity of kissing, he raised his head.

'There are so many ways I wish to take you I don't know where to begin.'

Heat burst beneath her skin and he laughed softly.

'You blush with the ease of an innocent.' He trailed his hand down her throat, lingering at her racing pulse, before it curved around one breast. 'It's almost enough to make me forget that you're not.' Again that bite, but less ferocious this time, his accent growing thicker as he bent his head and tongued her pulse.

She jerked against him, her fingers gliding over his warm skin of their own accord. 'On what basis do you form the opinion that I'm not?' she blurted before she lost her nerve.

He stilled, grey eyes turning that rare gunmetal shade that announced a dangerously heightened emotional state. His hand abandoned her breast and curled around her nape in an iron grip. 'What are you saying, Eva?' His voice was a hoarse rumble.

She licked nervous lips. 'That I don't want to be treated like I'm fragile...but I don't wish my first time to be without mercy either.'

He sucked in a stunned breath. 'Your *first... Madre di Dio.*' His gaze searched hers, his breathing growing increasingly erratic.

Slowly, he drew back from her, scouring her body from head to toe as if seeing her for the first time. He parted her thighs and she moved restlessly, helplessly, as his eyes lingered at her centre. Stilling her with one hand, he lowered his head and kissed her eyes, her mouth, her throat. Then lower until he reached her belly. He licked at her navel, then rained kisses on her quivering skin. Firm hands held her open, then his shoulders took over the job. Reading his intention, she raised her head from the pillow.

'Zaccheo.' She wasn't sure whether she was pleading for or rejecting what was coming.

He reared up for a second, his hands going to his hair to twist the long strands into an expert knot at the back of his head. The act was so unbelievably hot, her body threatened to melt into a useless puddle. Then he was back, broad shoulders easily holding her legs apart as he kissed his way down her inner thighs.

'I know what I crave most,' he muttered thickly. 'A taste of you.'

The first touch of his mouth at her core elicited a long, helpless groan from her. Her spine arched off the bed, her thighs shaking as fire roared through her body. He held her down and feasted on her, the varying friction from his mouth and beard adding an almost unholy pleasure that sent her soaring until a scream ripped from her throat and she fell off the edge of the universe.

She surfaced to feel his mouth on her belly, his hands trailing up her sides. That gunmetal shade of grey reflected deep possession as he rose above her and kissed her long and deep.

'Now, *il mio angelo*. Now I make you mine.'

He captured her hands above her head with one hand. The other reached between her thighs, gently massaging her core before he slid one finger inside her tight sheath. His groan echoed hers. Removing his finger, he probed her sex with his thick shaft, murmuring soft, soothing words as he pushed himself inside her.

'Easy, *dolcezza*.'

Another inch increased the burn, but the hunger rushing through her wouldn't be denied. Her fingers dug into his back, making him growl. 'Zaccheo, please.'

'*Sì*, let me please you.' He uttered a word that sounded like an apology, a plea.

Then he pushed inside her. The dart of pain engulfed her, lingered for a moment. Tears filled her eyes. Zaccheo cursed, then kissed them away, murmuring softly in Italian.

He thrust deeper, slowly filling her. Eva saw the strain etched on his face.

'Zaccheo?'

'I want this to be perfect for you.'

'It won't be unless you move, I suspect.'

That half-smile twitched, then stretched into a full, heart-stopping smile. Eva's eyes widened at the giddy dance her heart performed on seeing the wave of pleasure transform his face. Her own mouth curved in response and a feeling unfurled inside her, stealing her breath with its awesome power. Shakily, she raised her hand and touched his face, slid her fingers over his sensual mouth.

He moved. Withdrew and thrust again.

She gasped, her body caught in a maelstrom of sensation so turbulent, she feared she wouldn't emerge whole.

Slowly his smile disappeared, replaced by a wild, predatory hunger. He quickened the pace and her hands moved to his hair, slipping the knot free and burying her fingers in the thick, luxurious tresses. When her hips moved of their own accord, meeting him in an instinctive dance, he groaned deep and sucked one nipple into his mouth. Drowning in sensation, she felt her world begin to crumble. The moment he captured her twin nipple, a deep tremor started inside her. It built and built, then exploded in a shower of lights.

'Perfetto.'

Zaccheo sank his fingers into Eva's wild, silky hair, curbing the desire to let loose the primitive roar bubbling within him.

Mine. Finally, completely mine.

Instead he held her close until her breathing started to return to normal, then he flipped their positions and arranged her on top of him.

He was hard to the point of bursting, but he was determined to make this experience unforgettable for her. Seeing his ring on her finger, that primitive response rose again, stunning him with the strength of his desire to claim her.

His words on the plane slashed through his mind.

Sì, he *did* want this to work. Perhaps Eva had been right. Perhaps there was still time to salvage a piece of his soul...

Her eyes met his and a sensual smile curled her luscious mouth. Before he could instruct her, she moved, taking him deeper inside her before she rose. Knowing he was fast losing the ability to think, he met her second thrust. Her eyes widened, her skin flushing that alluring shade of pink as she chased the heady sensation. Within minutes, they were both panting.

Reaching down, he teased her with his thumb and watched

her erupt in bliss. Zaccheo followed her, his shout announcing the most ferocious release he'd experienced in his life.

Long after Eva had collapsed on top of him, and slipped
into an exhausted sleep, he lay awake.

Wondering why his world hadn't righted itself.

Wondering what the hell this meant for him.

CHAPTER TWELVE

EVA CAME AWAKE to find herself splayed on top of Zaccheo's body.

The sun remained high in the sky so she knew she hadn't slept for more than an hour or two. Nevertheless, the thought that she'd dropped into a coma straight after sex made her cringe.

She risked a glance and found grey eyes examining her with that half-smile she was growing to like a little more than she deemed wise.

He brushed a curl from her cheek and tucked it behind her ear. The gentleness in the act fractured her breathing.

'Ciao, dolcezza.'

'I didn't mean to fall asleep on you,' she said, then immediately felt gauche for not knowing the right after-sex etiquette.

He quirked a brow. 'Oh? Who did you mean to fall asleep on?' he asked.

She jerked up. 'No, that's not what I meant...' she started to protest, then stopped when she saw the teasing light in his eyes.

She started to settle back down, caught a glimpse of his chiselled pecs and immediately heat built inside her. A little wary of how quickly she was growing addicted to his body, she attempted to slide off him.

He stopped her with one hand at her nape, the other on her hip. The action flexed his arm and Eva's gaze was drawn to the tattoo banding his upper arm.

'Does this have a special meaning?'

His smile grew a little stiffer. 'It's a reminder not to accept less than I'm worth or compromise on what's important to me. And a reminder that, contrary to what the privileged would have us believe, all men are born equal. It's power that is wielded unequally.'

Eva thought of the circumstances that had brought her to this place, of the failings of her own family and the sadness she'd carried for so long, but now hoped to let go of.

'You wield more than enough share of power. Men cower before you.'

A frown twitched his forehead. 'If they do, it is their weakness, not mine.'

She gave an incredulous laugh. 'Are you saying you don't know you intimidate people with just a glance?'

His frown cleared. 'You're immune to this intimidation you speak of. To my memory, you've been disagreeable more often than not.'

She traced the outline of the tattoo, revelling in the smooth warmth of his skin. 'I've never been good at heeding bellowed commands.'

The hand on her hip tightened. 'I do not bellow.'

'Maybe not. But sometimes the effect is the same.'

She found herself flipped over onto her back, Zaccheo crouched over her like a lethal bird of prey. 'Is that why you hesitated as you walked down the aisle?' he asked in a harsh whisper. The look in his eyes was one of almost…hurt.

Quickly she shook her head. 'No, it wasn't.'

'Then what was it? You thought that I wasn't good enough, perhaps?' he pressed. And again she glimpsed a hint of vulnerability in his eyes that caught at a weak place in her heart.

She opened her mouth to *finally* tell him. To lay herself bare to the scathing rejection that would surely follow her confession.

The words stuck in her throat.

What she'd experienced in Zaccheo's bed had given her a taste that was unlike anything she'd ever felt before. The need to hold on to that for just a little while longer slammed into her, knocking aside her good intentions.

Eva knew she was playing with volcanic fire, that the eventual eruption would be devastating. But for once in her life, she wanted to be selfish, to experience a few moments of unfettered abandon. She could have that.

She'd sacrificed herself for this marriage, but in doing so she'd also been handed a say in when it ended.

And it would be sooner rather than later, because she couldn't stand in the way of what he wanted...what he'd been deprived of his whole life...a proper family of his own.

She also knew Zaccheo would want nothing to do with her once he knew the truth. Sure, he wasn't as monstrous as he would have others believe, but that didn't mean he would shackle himself to a wife who couldn't give him what he wanted.

She squashed the voice that cautioned she was naively burying her head in the sand.

Was it really so wrong if she chose to do it just for a little while?

Could she not live in bliss for a few days? Gather whatever memories she could and hang on to them for when the going got tough?

'Eva?'

'I had a father-daughter moment, plus bridal nerves,' she blurted. He raised a sceptical eyebrow and she smiled. 'Every woman is entitled to have a moment. Mine was thirty seconds of hesitation.'

'You remained frozen for five *minutes*,' he countered.

'Just time enough for anyone who'd been dozing off to wake up,' she responded, wide-eyed.

The tension slowly eased out of his body and his crooked smile returned. Relief poured through her and she fell into the punishing kiss he delivered to assert his displeasure at her hesitation.

She was clinging to him by the time he pulled away, and Eva was ready to protest when he swung out of bed. Her protest died when she got her first glimpse of his impressive manhood, and the full effect of the man attached to it.

Dry-mouthed and heart racing, she stared. And curled her fingers into the sheets to keep from reaching for him.

'If you keep looking at me like that, our shower will have to be postponed. And our lunch will go cold.'

A blush stormed up her face.

He laughed and scooped her up. 'But I'm glad that my body is not displeasing to you.'

She rolled her eyes. *As if.* 'False humility isn't an attractive trait, Zaccheo,' she chided as he walked them through a wide door and onto an outdoor bamboo-floored shower. Despite the rustic effects, the amenities were of the highest quality, an extra-wide marble bath sitting opposite a multi-jet shower, with a shelf holding rows upon rows of luxury bath oils and gels.

Above their heads, a group of macaws warbled throatily, then flew from one tree to the next, their stunning colours streaking through the branches.

As tropical paradises went, Eva was already sure this couldn't be topped, and she had yet to see the rest of it.

Zaccheo set her down and grabbed a soft washcloth. 'Complete compatibility in bed isn't a common thing, despite what magazines would have you believe,' he said.

'I wouldn't know.' There was no point pretending otherwise. He had first-hand knowledge of her innocence.

His eyes flared with possession as he turned on the jets and pulled her close.

'No, you wouldn't. And if that knowledge pleases me to the point of being labelled a caveman, then so be it.'

They ate a sumptuous lunch of locally caught fish served with pine-nut sauce and avocado salad followed by a serving of fruit and cheeses.

After lunch, Zaccheo showed her the rest of the house and the three-square-kilometre island. They finished the trek on the white sandy beach where a picnic had been laid out with champagne chilling in a silver bucket.

Eva popped a piece of papaya in her mouth and sighed at the beauty of the setting sun casting orange and purple streaks across the aquamarine water. 'I don't know how you can ever bear to leave this place.'

'I learned not to grow attached to things at an early age.'

The crisp reply had her glancing over at him. His shades were back in place so she couldn't read his eyes, but his body showed no signs of the usual forbidding *do not disturb* signs so she braved the question. 'Why?'

'Because it was better that way.'

She toyed with the stem of her champagne flute. 'But it's also a lonely existence.'

Broad shoulders lifted in an easy shrug. 'I had a choice of being lonely or just…solitary. I chose the latter.'

Her heart lurched at the deliberate absence of emotion from his voice. 'Zaccheo—'

He reared up from where he'd been lounging on his elbows, his mouth set in a grim line. 'Don't waste your time feeling sorry for me, *dolcezza*,' he said, his voice a hard snap that would've intimidated her, had she allowed it.

'I wasn't,' she replied. 'I'm not naive enough to imagine everyone has a rosy childhood. I know I didn't.'

'You mean the exclusive country-club memberships, the top boarding schools, the winters in Verbier weren't enough?' Despite the lack of contempt in his voice this time round, Eva felt sad that they were back in this place again.

'Don't twist my words. Those were just *things*, Zaccheo. And before you accuse me of being privileged, yes, I was. My childhood was hard, too, but I couldn't help the family I was born into any more than you could.'

'Was that why you moved out of Pennington Manor?'

'After my mother died, yes. Two against one became unbearable.'

'And the father-daughter moment you spoke of? Did that help?' he asked, watching her with a probing look.

A tiny bit of hope blossomed. 'Time will tell, I guess. Will you try the same with your mother and stepfather?'

'No. My mother didn't think I was worth anything. My stepfather agreed.'

Her heart twisted. 'Yet you've achieved success beyond most people's wildest dreams. Surely the lessons of your childhood should make you proud of who you are now, despite hating some aspects of your upbringing?'

'I detested all of mine,' he said with harsh finality. 'I wouldn't wish it on my worst enemy.'

The savage edge of pain in his voice made her shiver. She opened her mouth to ask him, but he surged to his feet.

'I don't wish to dwell in the past.' That half-smile flashed on and off. 'Not when I have a sunset as stunning as this and a wife to rival its beauty.' He plucked the glass from her hand and pulled her up.

Tucking her head beneath his chin, he enfolded her in his arms, one around her waist and the other across her shoulders. Eva knew it was a signal to drop the subject, but she couldn't let it go. Not just yet.

She removed his shades and stared into his slate-coloured eyes. 'For what it's worth, I gave away my country-club membership to my best friend, I hated boarding school, and I couldn't ski to save my life so I didn't even try after I turned ten. I didn't care about my pedigree, or who I was seen with. Singing and a family who cared for me were the only things that mattered. One helped me get through the other. So, you see, sometimes the grass *may* look greener on the other side, but most of the time it's just a trick of the light.'

Several emotions shifted within his eyes. Surprise. Shock. A hint of confusion. Then the deep arrogance of Zaccheo Giordano slid back into place.

'The sunset, *dolcezza*,' he said gruffly. 'You're missing it.'

* * *

The feeling of his world tilting out of control was escalating. And it spun harder out of sync the more he fought it.

Zaccheo had been certain he knew what drove Eva and her family. He'd been sure it was the same greed for power and prestige that had sent his father to a vicious and premature death. It was what had made his mother abandon her homeland to seek a rich husband, turn herself inside out for a man who looked down his nose at her son and ultimately made Clara Giordano pack her bags and move to the other side of the world.

But right from the start Eva had challenged him, forced him to confront his long-held beliefs. He hadn't needed to, of course. Oscar Pennington's actions had proven him right. Eva's own willingness to marry Fairfield for the sake of her family had cemented Zaccheo's belief.

And didn't you do the same thing?

He stared unseeing at the vivid orange horizon, his thoughts in turmoil.

He couldn't deny that the discovery of her innocence in bed had thrown him for a loop. Unsettled him in a way he hadn't been for a long time.

For as long as he could remember, his goal had been a fixed, tangible certainty. To place himself in a position where he erased any hint of neediness from his life, while delivering an abject lesson to those who thought themselves entitled and therefore could treat him as if he were common. A spineless fool who would prostrate himself for scraps from the high table.

He'd proven conclusively yesterday at his wedding reception that he'd succeeded beyond his wildest dreams. He'd watched blue-blooded aristocrats fall over themselves to win his favour.

And yet he'd found himself unsatisfied. Left with a hollow, bewildering feeling inside, as if he'd finally grasped the brass ring, only to find it was made of plastic.

It had left Zaccheo with the bitter introspection of whether a different, deeper goal lay behind the burning need to prove himself above the petty grasp for power and prestige.

The loneliness he'd so offhandedly dismissed had in fact eaten away at him far more effectively than his mother's rejection and the callous disregard his father had afforded him when he was alive.

Impatiently, he dismissed his jumbled feelings. He didn't do *feelings*. He *achieved*. He *bested*. And he *triumphed*.

One miscalculation didn't mean a setback. Finding out Eva had had no previous lovers had granted him an almost primitive satisfaction he wasn't going to bother to deny.

And if something came of this union sooner rather than later… His heart kicked hard.

Sliding a hand through her silky hair, he angled her face to his. Her beauty was undeniable. But he wouldn't be risking any more heart-to-hearts. She was getting too close, sliding under his skin to a place he preferred to keep out of bounds. A place he'd only examined when the cold damp of his prison cell had eroded his guard.

He was free, both physically and in guilt. He wouldn't return to that place. And he wouldn't allow her to probe further. Satisfied with his resolution, he kissed her sexy, tempting mouth until the need to breathe forced him to stop.

The sun had disappeared. Lights strung through the trees flickered on and he nodded to the member of staff who hovered nearby, ready to pack up their picnic.

He caught the glazed, flushed look on his wife's face and came to a sudden, extremely pleasing decision.

'Tonight, *il mio angelo*, we'll have an early night.'

The first week flew by in a dizzy haze of sun, sea, exquisite food, and making love. Lots and lots of making love.

Zaccheo was a fierce and demanding lover, but he gave so much more in return. And Eva was so greedy for everything he had to give, she wondered whether she was turning into a sex addict. She'd certainly acted like one this morning, when she'd initiated sex while Zaccheo had been barely awake. That her initiative had seemed to please him had been beside the point.

She'd examined her behaviour afterwards when Zaccheo had been summoned to an urgent phone call by Romeo.

This was supposed to be a moment out of time, a brief dalliance, which would end the moment she spilled her secret to him. And yet with each surrender of her body, she slid down a steeper slope, one she suspected would be difficult to climb back up. Because it turned out that, for her, sex wasn't a simple exchange of physical pleasure. With each act, she handed over a piece of herself to him that she feared she'd never reclaim.

And that more than anything made her fear for herself when this was over.

A breeze blew through an open window and Eva clutched the thin sarong she'd thrown over her bikini. Dark clouds were forming ominously over the island. Shivering, she watched the storm gather, wondering if it was a premonition for her own situation.

Lightning flashed, and she jumped.

'Don't worry, Mrs Eva.' Zaccheo's housekeeper smiled as she entered and turned on table lamps around the living room. 'The storm passes very quickly. The sun will be back out in no time.'

Eva smiled and nodded, but she couldn't shake the feeling that *her* storm wouldn't pass so quickly.

As intense rain pounded the roof she went in search of Zaccheo. Not finding him in his study, she climbed the stairs, her pulse already racing in anticipation as she went down the hallway.

She entered their dressing room and froze.

'What are you doing?' she blurted.

'I would've thought it was obvious, *dolcezza*.' He held clippers inches from his face.

'I can see what you're doing but...*why*?' she snapped. 'You already got rid of most of it for the wedding.' Her voice was clipped, a feeling she couldn't decipher moving through her.

Zaccheo raised an eyebrow, amusement mingled with something else as he watched her. 'I take it this look works for you?'

She swallowed twice before she could speak. When she finally deciphered the feeling coursing through her, she was so shocked and so afraid he would read her feelings, she glanced over his head.

'Yes. I prefer it,' she replied.

For several seconds he didn't speak. Her skin burned at his compelling stare. Schooling her features, she glanced into his eyes.

'Then it will remain untouched.' He set the clippers down and faced her.

Neither of them moved for several minutes. The storm raged outside, beating against the windows and causing the timber to creak.

'Come here, Eva.' Softly spoken, but a command nonetheless.

'I'm beginning to think those are your three favourite words.'

'They are only when you comply.'

She rolled her eyes, but moved towards him. He swivelled in his chair and pulled her closer, parting his thighs to situate her between them.

'Was that very hard to admit?' he rasped.

Her skin grew tight, awareness that she stood on a precipice whose depths she couldn't quite fathom shivering over her. 'No.'

He laughed. 'You're a pathetic liar. But I appreciate you finding the courage to ask for what you want.'

'An insult and a compliment?' she said lightly.

'I wouldn't want you to think me soft.' He caught her hands and placed them on his shoulders. 'You realise that

I'll require a reward for keeping myself this way for your pleasure?'

The way he mouthed *pleasure* made hot need sting between her thighs. Several weeks ago, she would've fought it. But Eva was fast learning it was no use. Her body was his slave to command as and when he wished. 'You got your stylists to prod and primp me into the image you wanted. I've earned the right to do the same to you.' Her fingers curled into the hair she would've wept to see shorn.

He smiled and relaxed in the chair. 'I thought being primped and plucked to perfection was every woman's wish?'

'You thought wrong. I was happy with the way I looked before.'

That wasn't exactly true. Although she'd loved her thick and wild hair, she had to admit it was much easier to tend now the wildness had been tamed a little. And she loved that she could brush the tresses without giving herself a headache. As for the luxurious body creams she'd been provided with, she marvelled at how soft and silky her skin felt now compared to before.

But she kept all of it to herself as he untied the knot in her sarong and let it fall away. 'You were perfect before. You're perfect now. And mine,' he breathed.

Within seconds, Eva was naked and craving what only he could give her, her eventual screams as loud as the storm raging outside.

CHAPTER THIRTEEN

'COME ON, we're taking the boat out today. As much as I'd like to keep you to myself, I think we need to see something of Rio before we leave tomorrow.'

Eva stopped tweaking the chorus of the melody she'd been composing and looked up as Zaccheo entered the living room.

The perverse hope that he would grow less breathtaking with each day was hopelessly thwarted. Dressed in khaki linen trousers and a tight white T-shirt with his hair loose around his shoulders, Zaccheo was so visually captivating, she felt the punch to her system each time she stared at him.

He noticed her staring and raised an eyebrow. Blushing, she averted her gaze to her tablet.

'Where are we going?' She tried for a light tone and breathed an inward sigh of relief when she succeeded.

'To Ilha São Gabriel, three islands away. It's a tourist hotspot, but there are some interesting sights to see there.' He crouched before her, his gaze going to the tablet. Reaching out, he scrolled through her compositions, his eyes widening at the three dozen songs contained in the file.

'You wrote all these?' he asked.

She nodded, feeling self-conscious as he paused at a particularly soul-baring ballad about unrequited love and rejection. She'd written that one a week after Zaccheo had gone to prison. 'I've been composing since I was sixteen.'

His eyes narrowed on her face. 'You've had two million pounds in your bank account for over a year and a half, which I'm guessing is your shareholder dividend from your father's deal on my building?'

Warily, she nodded.

'That would've been more than enough money to pursue your music career without needing to work. So why didn't you use it?' he queried.

She tried to shrug the question away, but he caught her chin in his hand. 'Tell me,' he said.

'I suspected deep down that the deal was tainted. I hated doubting my father's integrity, but I could never bring myself to use the money. It didn't feel right.' Being proved right had brought nothing but hurt.

He watched her for a long time, a puzzled look on his face before he finally nodded. 'How was your session with Ziggy Preston?' he asked.

She saw nothing of the sour expression he'd sported that night in the club. 'Surprisingly good, considering I'd thought he'd have me on the blacklist of every music producer after your behaviour.'

An arrogant smile stretched his lips. 'They'd have had to answer to me had they chosen that unfortunate path. You're seeing him again?'

She nodded. 'When we get back.'

'Bene.' He rose and held out his hand.

She slipped her feet into one of the many stylish sandals now gracing her wardrobe and he led her outside to the jetty.

Climbing on board, he placed her in front of the wheel and stood behind her. She looked around, expecting Zaccheo's right-hand man to be travelling with them. 'Isn't Romeo coming?'

'He had business to take care of in Rio. He'll meet us there.'

The trip took twenty-five minutes, and Eva understood why the Ilha São Gabriel was so popular when she saw it. The island held a mountain, on top of which a smaller version of the Cristo Redentor in Rio had been erected. Beneath the statue, bars, restaurants, parks and churches flowed right down to the edge of a mile-long beach.

Zaccheo directed her to motor past the busy beach and round the island to a quieter quay where they moored the boat. 'We're starting our tour up there.' He pointed to a quaint little building set into the side of a hill about a quarter of a mile up a steep path.

She nodded and started to walk up when she noticed Romeo a short distance away. He nodded a greeting but didn't join them as they headed up. The other man's watchfulness made Eva frown.

'Something on your mind?' Zaccheo asked.

'I was just wondering...what's the deal with Romeo?'

'He's many things.'

'That's not really an answer.'

Zaccheo shrugged. 'We work together, but I guess he's a confidant.'

'How long have you known him?'

When Zaccheo pulled his shades from the V of his T-shirt and placed them on, she wondered whether she'd strayed into forbidden territory. But he answered, 'We met when I was thirteen years old.'

Her eyes rounded in surprise. 'In London?'

'In Palermo.'

'So he's your oldest friend?'

Zaccheo hesitated for a second. 'Our relationship is complicated. Romeo sees himself as my protector. A role I've tried to dissuade him from to no avail.'

Her heart caught. 'Protector from what?'

His mouth twitched. 'He seems to think you're a handful that he needs to keep an eye on.'

She looked over her shoulder at the quiet, brooding man.

'My father worked for his father,' he finally answered.

'In what capacity?'

'As whatever he wanted him to be. My father didn't discriminate as long as he was recognised for doing the job. He would do anything from carrying out the trash to kneecapping a rival gang's members to claiming another man's bastard child so his boss didn't have to. No job was too small or large,' he said with dry bitterness.

The blood drained from her face. 'Your father worked for the *Mafia*?'

His jaw clenched before he jerked out a nod. 'Romeo's father was a *don* and my father one of his minions. His role was little more than drudge work, but he acted as if he was serving the Pope himself.'

She glanced over her shoulder at Romeo, her stomach dredging with intense emotions she recognised as anguish— even without knowing what Zaccheo was about to divulge.

'That bastard child you mentioned...'

He nodded. 'Romeo. His father had an affair with one of his many mistresses. His mother kept him until he became too much of a burden. When he was thirteen, she dumped him on his father. He didn't want the child, so he asked my father to *dispose* of him. My father, eager to attain recognition at all costs, brought the child home to my mother. She refused but my father wouldn't budge. They fought every day for a month until she ended up in hospital. It turned out she was pregnant. After that she became even more adamant about having another woman's child under her roof. When she lost her baby, she blamed my father and threatened to leave. My father, probably for the only time in his life, decided to place someone else's needs above his ambition. He tried to return Romeo to his father, who took grave offence. He had my father beaten to death. And I...' his face tightened '...I went from having a friend, a mother and father, and a brother or sister on the way, to having nothing.'

Eva frowned. 'But your mother—'

'Had hated being the wife of a mere gofer. My father's death bought her the fresh start she craved, but she had to contend with a child who reminded her of a past she detested. She moved to England a month after he died and married a man who hated the sight of me, who judged me because of who my father was and believed my common blood was an affront to his distinguished name.' The words were snapped out in a staccato narrative, but she felt the anguished intensity behind them.

Eva swallowed hard. Stepping close, she laid her head on his chest. 'I'm so sorry, Zaccheo.'

His arms tightened around her for a heartbeat before he pulled away and carried on up the steps. 'I thought Romeo had died that night, too, until he found me six years ago.'

She glanced at Romeo and her heart twisted for the pain the unfortunate friends had gone through.

They continued up the hill in silence until they reached the building.

They entered the cool but dim interior and as her eyes adjusted to the dark she was confronted by a stunning collection of statues. Most were made of marble, but one or two were sculpted in white stone.

'Wow, these are magnificent.'

'A local artist sculpted all the patron saints and donated them to the island over fifty years ago.'

They drifted from statue to statue, each work more striking than the last. When they walked through an arch, he laced his fingers with hers. 'Come, I'll show you the most impressive one. According to the history, the artist sculpted them in one day.'

Smiling, she let him tug her forward. She gasped at the double-figured display of St Anne and St Gerard. 'Patron saints of motherhood and fertility…' She stopped reading as her heart dropped to her stomach.

Zaccheo traced a forefinger down her cheek. 'I can't wait to feel our child kick in your belly,' he murmured.

A vice gripped her heart, squeezed until it threatened to stop beating. 'Zaccheo—'

His finger stopped her. 'I meant what I said, Eva. We can make this work. And we may not have had the best of role models in parents, but we know which mistakes to avoid. That's a good basis for our children, *si*?' he asked, his tone gentle, almost hopeful.

She opened her mouth, but no words formed. Because the truth she'd been hiding from suddenly reared up and slapped her in the face.

Zaccheo wanted children, not as a tool for revenge, but for himself. The man who'd known no love growing up wanted a family of his own.

And she'd led him on, letting him believe he could have it with her. The enormity of her actions rocked her to the core, robbing her of breath.

'Eva? What's wrong?' he asked with a frown.

She shook her head, her eyes darting frantically around the room.

'You're as pale as a ghost, *dolcezza*. Talk to me!'

Eva struggled to speak around the misery clogging her throat. 'I...I'm okay.'

His frown intensified. 'You don't look okay. Do you want to leave?'

She grasped the lifeline. 'Yes.'

'Okay, let's go.'

They emerged into bright sunlight. Eva took a deep breath, which did absolutely nothing to restore the chaos fracturing her mind.

The urge to confess *now*, spill her secret right then and there, powered through her. But it was neither the time nor the place. A group of tourist students had entered the room and the place was getting busier by the second.

Zaccheo led her down the steps. He didn't speak, but his concerned gaze probed her.

The island seemed twice as crowded by the time they descended the hill. The midday sun blazed high and sweat trickled down her neck as they navigated human traffic on the main promenade. When Zaccheo steered her to a restaurant advertising fresh seafood, Eva didn't complain.

Samba music blared from the speakers, thankfully negating the need for conversation. Sadly it didn't free her from her thoughts, not even when, after ordering their food, Zaccheo moved his chair closer, tugged her into his side and trailed his hand soothingly through her hair.

It was their last day in Rio. Possibly their last as husband and wife. Her soul mourned what she shouldn't have craved.

Unbearable agony ripped through her. She'd been living in a fool's paradise. Especially since she'd told herself it wouldn't matter how much time passed without her telling Zaccheo.

It mattered very much. She'd heard his pain when he'd recounted his bleak childhood. With each day that had passed without her telling him she couldn't help him realise his dream, she'd eroded any hope that he would understand why she'd kept her secret from him.

A moan ripped from her throat and she swayed in her seat. Zaccheo tilted her face to his and she read the worry in his eyes.

'Do you feel better?'

'Yes, much better.'

'*Bene*, then perhaps you'd like to tell me what's going on?' he asked.

She jerked away, her heart hammering. 'I got a little light-headed, that's all.'

His frown returned and Eva held her breath. She was saved when Romeo entered. 'Everything all right?' he asked.

Romeo's glance darted to her. The knowledge in his eyes froze her insides, but he said nothing, directing his gaze back to his friend.

Zaccheo nodded. '*Sì*. We'll see you back at Paraíso.'

The moment he left, Zaccheo lowered his head and kissed her, not the hungry devouring that tended to overtake them whenever they were this close, but a gentle, reverent kiss.

In that moment, Eva knew she'd fallen in love with him.

And that she would lose the will to live the moment she walked away from him.

Their food arrived and they ate. She refused coffee and the slice of *chocotorta* the waiter temptingly offered. Zaccheo ordered an espresso, shooting her another concerned glance. Praying he wouldn't press her to reveal what was wrong just yet, she laid her head on his shoulder and buried her face in his throat, selfishly relishing the moment. She would never get a moment like this once they returned to Casa do Paraíso. He placed a gentle kiss on her forehead and agony moved through her like a living entity.

You brought this on yourself. No use crying now.

She started as the group they'd met on their exit from the museum entered the restaurant. Within minutes, someone had started the karaoke machine. The first attempt, sung atrociously to loud jeers, finished as the waiter returned with Zaccheo's espresso.

Eva straightened in her seat, watching the group absently as each member refused to take the mic. The leader cast his eyes around the room, met Eva's gaze and made a beeline for her.

'No.' She shook her head when he reached her and offered the mic.

He clasped his hands together. *'Por favor,'* he pleaded.

She opened her mouth to refuse, then found herself swallowing her rebuttal. She glanced at Zaccheo. He regarded her steadily, his face impassive. And yet she sensed something behind his eyes, as if he didn't know what to make of her mood.

She searched his face harder, wanting him to say something, *anything*, that would give her even the tiniest hope that what she had to tell him wouldn't break the magic they'd found on his island. Wouldn't break *her*.

In a way it was worse when he offered her that half-smile. Recently his half-smiles had grown genuine, were often a precursor to the blinding smiles that stole her breath…made her heart swell to bursting.

The thought that they would soon become a thing of the past had her surging to her feet, blindly striding for the stage to a round of applause she didn't want.

All Eva wanted in that moment was to drown in the oblivion of music.

She searched through the selection until she found a song she knew by heart, one that had spoken to her the moment she'd heard it on the radio.

She sang the first verse with her eyes shut, yearning for the impossible. She opened her eyes for the second verse. She could never tell Zaccheo how she felt about him, but she could sing it to him. Her eyes found his as she sang the last line.

His gaze grew hot. Intense. Her pulse hammered as she sang the third verse, offering her heart, her life to him, all the while knowing he would reject it once he knew.

She stifled a sob as the machine clicked to an end. She started to step off the stage, but the group begged for another song.

Zaccheo rose and moved towards her. They stared at each other as the clamouring grew louder. Her breath caught when the emotion in his eyes altered, morphing into that darker hue that held a deeper meaning.

He wasn't angry. Or ruthlessly commanding her to bend to his will. Or even bitter and hurt, as he'd been on the hill.

There was none of that in his expression. This ferocity was different, one that made her world stop.

Until she shook herself back to reality. She was grasping at straws, stalling with excuses and foolish, reckless hope. She might have fallen in love with Zaccheo, but nothing he'd said or done had indicated he returned even an iota of what she felt. Their relationship had changed from what it'd been in the beginning, but she couldn't lose sight of *why* it'd begun in the first place. Or why she couldn't let it continue.

Heavy-hearted, she turned back to the machine. She'd seen the song earlier and bypassed it, because she hadn't been ready to say goodbye.

But it was time to end this. Time to accept that there was no hope.

Something was wrong. It'd been since they'd walked down the hill.

But for once in his life, he was afraid to confront a problem head-on because he was terrified the results would be unwelcome. So he played worst-case scenarios in his head.

Had he said or done something to incite this troubled look on Eva's face? Had his confession on the hill reminded her that he wasn't the man she would've chosen for herself? A wave of something close to desolation rushed over him. He clenched his jaw against the feeling. Would it really be the end of the world if Eva decided she didn't want him? The affirmative answer echoing through him made him swallow hard.

He discarded that line of thought and chose another, dissecting each moment he'd spent with her this afternoon.

He'd laid himself bare, something he'd never done until recently. She hadn't shown pity or disgust for the debasing crimes his father had committed, or for the desperately lonely child he'd been. Yet again she'd only showed compassion. Pain for the toll his jagged upbringing had taken on him.

And the songs…what had they meant, especially the second one, the one about saying *goodbye*? He'd witnessed the agony in her eyes while she'd sung that one. As if her heart was broken—

A knock came at his study door, where he'd retreated to pace after they'd returned and Eva had expressed the need for a shower. Alone.

'Zaccheo?'

He steeled himself to turn around, hoping against hope that the look on her face would be different. That she would smile and everything would return to how it was before they'd gone on that blasted trip.

But it wasn't. And her next words ripped through him with the lethal effect of a vicious blade.

'Zaccheo, we need to talk.'

CHAPTER FOURTEEN

EVERY WORD SHE'D practised in the shower fled her head as Eva faced him. Of course, her muffled sobs had taken up a greater part of the shower so maybe she hadn't got as much practice in as she'd thought.

'I...' Her heart sank into her stomach when a forbidding look tightened his face. 'I can't stay married to you.'

For a moment he looked as if she'd punched him hard in the solar plexus, then ripped his heart out while he struggled to breathe. Gradually his face lost every trace of pain and distress. Hands shoved deep in his pockets, he strolled to where she stood, frozen inside the doorway.

'Was this your plan all along?' he bit out, his eyes arctic. 'To wait until I'd spoken on your father's behalf and he was safe from prosecution before you asked for a divorce?'

She gasped. 'You did that? When?' she asked, but his eyes poured scorn on her question.

'Is being married to me that abhorrent to you, Eva? So much so you couldn't even wait until we were back in London?'

'No! Believe me, Zaccheo, that's not it.'

'*Believe* you? Why should I? When you're not even prepared to give us a chance?' He veered sharply away from her and strode across the room, his fingers spiking through his hair before he reversed course and stopped in front of her once more. 'What I don't understand is why. Did I do something? Say something to make you think I wouldn't want this relationship to work?'

The confirmation that this marriage meant more to him was almost too hard to bear.

'Zaccheo, please listen to me. It's not you, it's—'

His harsh laughter echoed around the room. 'Are you *seriously* giving me that line?'

Her fists balled. 'For once in your life, just shut up and listen! I can't have children,' she blurted.

'You've already used that one, *dolcezza*, but you signed along the dotted line agreeing to my clause, remember? So try again.'

Misery quivered through her stomach. 'It's true I signed the agreement, but I lied to you. I *can't* have children, Zaccheo. I'm infertile.'

He sucked in a hoarse breath and reeled backwards on his heels. 'Excuse me?'

'I tried to tell you when I first saw the clause, but you wouldn't listen. You'd made up your mind that I'd use any excuse not to marry you because I didn't want you.'

The stunned look morphed into censure. 'Then you should've put me straight.'

'How? Would you have believed me if I'd told you about my condition? Without evidence to back it up? Or perhaps I should've told Romeo or your PA since they had more access to you than I did in the week before the wedding?'

He looked at her coldly. 'If your conscience stung you so deeply the first time round, why did you change your mind?'

Her emotions were raw enough for her to instinctively want to protect herself. But what did she have to lose? Zaccheo would condemn her actions regardless of whether she kept her innermost feelings to herself or not. And really, how much worse could this situation get? Her heart was already in shreds.

She met his gaze head on. 'You know I lost my mother to cancer when I was eighteen. She was diagnosed when I was sixteen. For two years we waited, hoping for the best, fearing the worst through each round of chemo. With each treatment that didn't work we knew her time was growing shorter. Knowing it was coming didn't make it any easier. Her death ripped me apart.' She stopped and gathered her courage. 'My father has been suffering stress attacks in the last couple of months.' She risked a glance and saw his brows clamped in a forbidding frown. 'He collapsed on Friday after you called to tell him the wedding was off.'

Zaccheo's mouth compressed, but a trace of compassion flashed through his eyes. 'And you blame me? Is that what this is all about?'

'No, I don't. We both know that the blame for our current circumstances lies firmly with my father.' She stopped and licked her lips. 'He may have brought this on himself, but the stress was killing him, Zaccheo. I've watched one parent die, helpless to do anything but watch them fade away. Condemn me all you want, but I wasn't going to stand by and let my father worry himself to death over what he'd done. And I didn't do it for my family name or my blasted *pedigree*. I did it because that's what you do for the people you love.'

'Even when they don't love you back?' he sneered, his voice indicating hers was a foolish feeling. 'Even when they treat you like an afterthought for most of your life?'

Sadness engulfed her. 'You can't help who you love. Or choose who will love you back.'

His eyes met hers for a charged second, before his nostrils flared. 'But you can choose to tell the truth no matter how tough the telling of it is. You can choose *not* to start a marriage based on lies.'

Regret crawled across her skin. 'Yes. And I'm sorry—'

His hand slashed through air, killing off her apology. Walking around her, he slammed the door shut and jerked his chin towards the sofa. He waited until she'd sat down, then prowled in front of her.

'Tell me of this condition you have.'

Eva stared at her clasped hands because watching his face had grown unbearable. 'It's called endometriosis.' She gave him the bare facts, unwilling to linger on the subject and prolong her heartache. 'It started just before I went to university, but, with everything going on with my mother, I didn't pay enough attention to it. I thought it was just something that would right itself eventually. But the pain got worse. One day I collapsed and was rushed to hospital. The diagnosis was made.' She stopped, then made herself go on. 'The doctor said the…scarring was too extensive…that I would never conceive naturally.'

She raised her head and saw that he'd stopped prowling and taken a seat opposite her with his elbows on his knees. 'Go on,' he bit out.

Eva shrugged. 'What else is there to add?' She gave a hollow laugh. 'I never thought I'd be in a position where the one thing I couldn't give would be the difference between having the future I want and the one I'd have to settle for. You accused me of starting this marriage based on lies, but I didn't know you wanted a real marriage. You did all this to get back at my father, remember?'

'So you never sought a second opinion?' he asked stonily, as if she hadn't mentioned the shifted parameters of their marriage.

'Why would I? I'd known something was wrong. Having the doctor confirm it merely affirmed what I already suspected. What was the point of putting myself through further grief?'

Zaccheo jerked to his feet and began prowling again. The set of his shoulders told her he was holding himself on a tight leash.

Minutes ticked by and he said nothing. The tension increased until she couldn't stand it any more. 'You can do whatever you want with me, but I want your word that you won't go after my family because of what I've done.'

He froze, his eyes narrowing to thin shards of ice. 'You think I want you to martyr yourself on some noble pyre for my sick satisfaction?'

She jumped to her feet. 'I don't know! You're normally so quick to lay down your demands. Or throw out orders and expect them to be followed. So tell me what you want.'

That chilling half-smile returned with a vengeance. 'What I want is to leave this place. There's really no point staying, is there, since the honeymoon is well and truly over?'

The flight back was markedly different from the outbound journey. The moment Zaccheo immersed himself in his work, she grabbed her tablet and locked herself in the bedroom.

She threw herself on the bed and sobbed long and hard into the pillow. By the time the plane landed in London, she was completely wrung out. Exhaustion seeped into her very bones and all she wanted was to curl into a foetal position and wish the world away.

She sank further into grey gloom when she descended the steps of the aircraft to find Zaccheo's limo waiting on the tarmac, along with a black SUV.

Zaccheo, wearing a black and navy pinstriped suit, stopped next to her, his expression remote and unfriendly.

'I'm heading to the office. Romeo will drive you to the penthouse.'

He strode to the SUV and drove off.

Eva realised then that throughout their conversation on the island, she'd made the same mistake as when she'd foolishly disclosed her condition before. She'd allowed herself to *hope* that the condition fate had bestowed on her wouldn't matter to that one *special person*. That somehow *love* would find a way.

A sob bubbled up her chest and she angrily swallowed it down.

Grow up, Eva. You're letting the lyrics of your songs cloud your judgement.

'Eva?' Romeo waited with the car door open.

She hastily averted her gaze from the censure in his eyes and slid in.

The penthouse hadn't changed, and yet Eva felt as if she'd lived a lifetime since she was last here.

After unpacking and showering, she trailed from room to room, feeling as if some tether she hadn't known she was tied to had been severed. When she rushed to the door for the third time, imagining she'd heard the keycard activate, she grabbed her tablet and forced herself to work on her compositions.

But her heart wasn't in it. Her mood grew bleaker when Romeo found her curled on the sofa and announced that Zaccheo wouldn't be home for dinner either tonight or the next two weeks, because he'd returned to Oman.

The days bled together in a dull grey jumble. Determined not to mope—because after all she'd been here before—Eva returned to work.

She took every spare shift available and offered herself for overtime without pay.

But she refused to sing.

Music had ceased to be the balm she'd come to rely on. Her heart only yearned for one thing. Or *one man*. And he'd made it abundantly clear that he didn't want her.

Because two weeks stretched to four, then six with no word from Zaccheo, and no answer to her phone calls.

At her lowest times, Eva hated herself for her lethargy, for not moving out of the penthouse. For sitting around, wishing for a miracle that would never materialise.

But the thought of flat-hunting, or, worse, moving back to Pennington Manor, filled her with a desperate heartache that nothing seemed to ease.

Romeo had brought her coffee this morning at the breakfast table. The pitying look he'd cast her had been the final straw.

'If you have something to say, just say it, Romeo.'

'You're not a weak woman. One of you has to take the situation in hand sooner or later,' he'd replied.

'Fine, but he won't return my calls so give him a message from me, will you?'

He'd nodded in that solemn way of his. 'Of course.'

'Tell him I'm fast reaching my tolerance level for his stupid silence. He can stay in Oman for the rest of his life for all I care. But he shouldn't expect to find me here when he deigns to return.'

That outburst had been strangely cathartic. She'd called her ex-landlady and discovered her flat was still unlet. After receiving a hefty payday from Zaccheo, the old woman hadn't been in a hurry to interview new tenants. She'd invited Eva to move back whenever she wanted.

Curiously, that announcement hadn't made her feel better—

'You've been cleaning that same spot for the last five minutes.'

Eva started and glanced down. 'Oh.'

Sybil, Siren's unflappable manageress, eyed her. 'Time for a break.'

'I don't need a—'

'Sorry, love,' Sybil said firmly. 'Orders from above. The new owner was very insistent. You take a break now or I get docked a week's wages.'

Eva frowned. 'Are you serious? Do we know who this new owner is?'

Sybil's eyes widened. 'You don't know?' When she shook her head, the manageress shrugged. 'Well, I'm not one to spread gossip. Shoo! Go put your feet up for a bit. I'll finish up here.'

Eva reluctantly handed over the cleaning supplies. She turned and stopped as the doors swung open and Ziggy Preston walked in.

The smile she tried for failed miserably. 'Ziggy, hello.'

He smiled. 'I heard you were back in town.'

She couldn't summon the curiosity to ask how he knew. 'Oh?'

'You were supposed to call when you got back. I hope that doesn't mean you've signed up with someone else? Because that'd devastate me,' he joked.

Eva tried for another smile. Failed again. 'I didn't sign with anyone, and I don't think I will.'

His face fell. 'Why not?'

She had a thousand and one reasons. But only one that mattered. And she wasn't about to divulge it to another soul. 'I've decided to give the music thing a break for a while.' Or for ever, depending on whether she felt anything but numb again.

Ziggy shoved his hands into his coat pocket, his features pensive.

'Listen, I was supposed to do a session with one of my artists tomorrow afternoon, but they cancelled. Come to the studio, hang out for a while. You don't have to sing if you don't want to. But come anyway.'

She started to shake her head, then stopped. It was her day off tomorrow. The extra shift she'd hoped to cover had suddenly been filled. She could either occupy herself at Ziggy's studio or wander Zaccheo's penthouse like a lost wraith, pining for what she could never have. 'Okay.'

'Great!' He handed her another business card, this one with his private number scribbled on the back, and left.

A couple of months ago, being pursued by a top music producer would've been a dream come true. And yet, Eva could barely summon the enthusiasm to dress the next day, especially when Romeo confirmed he'd given Zaccheo her message but had no reply for her.

Jaw clenched, she pulled on her jeans and sweater, determined not to succumb to the unending bouts of anguish that had made her throw up this morning after her conversation with Romeo.

She wasn't a pearl-clutching Victorian maiden, for heaven's sake!

Her life might *feel* as if it were over, but she'd been through the wringer more than once in her life. She'd survived her diagnosis. She'd survived her mother's death. Despite the odds, she'd mended fences with her father and sister.

Surely she could survive decimating her heart on a love that had been doomed from the start?

Deliberately putting a spring in her step, she arrived at Ziggy's studio in a different frame of mind. Looking around, she repeated to herself that *this* was a tangible dream. Something she could hang on to once Zaccheo returned and she permanently severed the ties that had so very briefly bound them.

Eva was sure she was failing in her pep talk to herself when Ziggy gave up after a third attempt to get her to sample an upbeat pop tune.

'Okay, shall we try one of yours?' he suggested with a wry smile.

Half-heartedly, she sifted through her list, then paused, her heart picking up its sluggish beat as she stared at the lyrics to the song she'd composed that last morning on the island.

'This one,' she murmured.

At Ziggy's nod, she sang the first line.

His eyes widened. 'Wow.' Nodding to the sound booth, he said, 'I'd love to hear the whole thing if you're up to it?'

Eva thought of the raw lyrics, how they offered love, pleaded for for ever and accepted any risks necessary, and breathed deeply.

If this was what it took to start healing herself, then so be it. 'Sure.'

She was singing the final notes when an electrifying wave of awareness swept over her. Her gaze snapped up to the viewing gallery above the booth, where she knew music moguls sometimes listened in on artists. Although the mirrored glass prevented her from seeing who occupied it, she swore she could smell Zaccheo's unique scent.

'Are you okay?' Ziggy asked.

She nodded absently, her gaze still on the gallery window.

'Can you sing the last two lines again?'

'Umm…yes,' she mumbled.

She really was losing it. If she couldn't sing a song she'd written with Zaccheo in mind without imagining she could feel him, smell him, she was in deep trouble. Because as she worked through the other songs Ziggy encouraged her to re-cord, Eva realised all her songs were somehow to do with the man who'd taken her heart prisoner.

She left the studio in a daze and got into the waiting limo. Physically and emotionally drained, she couldn't connect two thoughts together. When she finally accepted what she needed to do, she turned to Romeo.

'Can you take me to Zaccheo's office, please?'

He looked up from the laptop he'd been working on. After a few probing seconds, he nodded.

A wave of dizziness hit her as they waited for the lift at GWI. She ignored the curious glances, and concentrated on staying upright, putting one foot in front of the other as she made her way down the plushly decorated corridor to Zac-cheo's office.

Anyetta's coolly professional demeanour visibly altered when she saw Eva, then turned to shock as her gaze travelled from her head to her toes.

Eva wanted to laugh, but she couldn't be sure she wouldn't dissolve into hysteria. When Anyetta stood, Eva waved her away.

'I know he's not in. I was hoping *you* would email him for me.'

'But—'

'It won't take long, I promise.'

The tall brunette looked briefly bewildered, but her fea-tures settled back into serene composure and she sat down.

'Mark it *urgent*. Presumably, you can tell when he opens emails from you?' Eva asked.

Warily, Zaccheo's PA nodded.

'Good.' Eva approached, pushing back the errant curls obscuring her vision. She folded her arms around her middle and prayed for just a few more minutes of strength.

Anyetta's elegant fingers settled on the keyboard.
Eva cleared her throat.

Zaccheo.
Since you refuse to engage with me, I can only conclude that I'm free of my obligations to you. To that end, I'd be grateful if you would take the appropriate steps to end this marriage forthwith. My family lawyers will be on standby when you're ready, but I'd be obliged if you didn't leave it too late. I refuse to put my life on hold for you, so take action or I will.
For the record, I won't be accepting any of the monetary compensation offered, nor will I be seeking anything from you, except my freedom. If you choose to pursue my family, then you'll do so without my involvement, because I've done my duty to my family and I'm moving on. I won't let you use me as a pawn in your vendetta against my father.
You're aware of the state of my father's health, so I hope you'll choose mercy over retribution.
Regardless of your decision, I'll be moving out of the penthouse tomorrow.
Please don't contact me.
Eva.

'Send it, please,' she said.

Anyetta clicked the button, then looked up. 'He just opened it.'

Eva nodded jerkily. 'Thank you.'

She walked out with scalding tears filling her eyes. A solid presence registered beside her and when Romeo took her arm, Eva didn't protest.

At the penthouse, she dropped her bag in the hallway, tugged off her boots and coat as her vision greyed. She made it into bed as her legs gave way and she curled, fully clothed, into a tight ball. Her last thought before blessed oblivion claimed her was that she'd done it.

She'd survived her first hour with a heart broken into a million tiny pieces. If there was any justice, she might just make it through the rest of her life with a shredded heart.

CHAPTER FIFTEEN

IN THE SPLIT SECOND before wakefulness hit, Eva buried her nose in the pillow that smelled so much like Zaccheo she groaned with pure, incandescent happiness.

Reality arrived with searing pain so acute, she cried out.

'Eva.'

She jolted upright at the sound of her name. Jagged thoughts pierced her foggy brain like shards of bright light through glass.

She was no longer in her own suite, but in Zaccheo's.

Her clothes were gone, and she was stripped down to her bra and panties.

Zaccheo was sitting in an armchair next to the bed, his eyes trained on her.

And he was clean-shaven.

His thick stubble was gone, his hair trimmed into a short, neat style that left his nape bare.

Despite his altered appearance, his living, breathing presence was far too much to bear. She jerked her head away, stared down at the covers she clutched like a lifeline.

'What are you doing here?' she asked.

'You summoned me. So here I am,' he stated.

She shook her head. 'Please. Don't make it sound as if I have any power over your actions. If I did you would've answered my numerous phone calls like a normal person. And that email wasn't a summons. It was a statement of intent, hardly demanding your presence.'

'Nevertheless, since you went to so much trouble to make sure it reached me, I thought it only polite to answer it in person.'

'Well, you needn't have bothered,' she threw back hotly,

'especially since we both know you don't have a polite bone in your body. Things like *consideration* and *courtesy* are alien concepts to you.'

He looked perturbed by her outburst. Which made her want to laugh. And cry. And scream. 'Are you going to sit there with that insulting look that implies I'm out of my mind?'

'You must forgive me if that's what my expression implies. I meant to wear a look that says I was hoping for a civilised conversation.'

She threw out her hands. 'You have a damned nerve, do you know that? I…' She stopped, her eyes widening in alarm as an unpleasant scent hit her nostrils. Swivelling, she saw the breakfast tray containing scrambled eggs, smoked pancetta, coffee, and the buttered brioche she loved.

Correction. She'd *once* loved.

Shoving the covers aside, she lunged for the bathroom, uncaring that she was half-naked and looked like a bedraggled freak. All she cared about was making it to the porcelain bowl in time.

She vomited until she collapsed against the shower stall, desperately catching her breath. When Zaccheo crouched at her side, she shut her eyes. 'Please, Zaccheo. Go away.'

He pressed a cool towel to her forehead, her eyelids, her cheeks. 'A lesser man might be decimated at the thought that his presence makes you physically ill,' he murmured gravely.

Her snort grated her throat. 'But you're not a lesser man, of course.'

He shrugged. 'I'm saved by Romeo's report that you've been feeling under the weather recently.'

Eva opened her eyes, looked at him, then immediately wished she hadn't. She'd thought his beard and long mane made him gloriously beautiful, but the sight of his chiselled jaw, the cut of his cheekbones, and the fully displayed sensual lips was almost blinding.

'I can't do this.' She tried to stand and collapsed back against the stall.

With a muttered oath, he scooped her up in his arms and strode to the vanity. Setting her down, he handed her a tooth-brush and watched as she cleaned her teeth.

Eva told herself the peculiar look turning his eyes that gunmetal shade meant nothing. Zaccheo had probably come to ensure she vacated his penthouse before succumbing to whatever was ailing her.

Steeling her spine, she rinsed her mouth. He reached for her as she moved away from the vanity, but she sidestepped him, her heart banging against her ribs. 'I can walk on my own two feet.'

Zaccheo watched her go, her hips swaying in that imper-tinent, yet utterly sexy way that struck pure fire to his libido.

He slowly followed, paused in the doorway and watched her pace the bedroom.

Although he'd primed himself for her appearance, he hadn't been quite prepared for when he'd finally returned to the penthouse last night and found her asleep in her suite. All the excuses he'd given himself for staying away had crumbled to dust.

As he'd stood over her, his racing heart had only been able to acknowledge one thing—that he'd missed her more than his brain could accurately fathom. He'd thought the daily reports on her movements would be enough. He'd thought buying Siren and ensuring she didn't overwork her-self, or silently watching her from the gallery at Preston's studio yesterday, listening to her incredible voice, would be enough.

It wasn't until he'd received her email that his world had stopped, and he'd forced himself to face the truth.

He was nothing without her.

For the last six weeks he'd woken to a tormenting exis-tence each morning. Each time, something had broken in-side him. Something that would probably slot neatly under the banner of heartache. It had nothing to do with the lone-liness that had plagued his childhood and led him to believe he needed a family to soothe the ache. It had nothing to do with the retribution he was no longer interested in exacting from Oscar Pennington.

It had everything to do with Eva. Flashes of her had struck him at the most inappropriate times—like the brightness of her smile when he was involved in tense negotiation. The feeling of being deep inside her when he was teetering on the edge of a platform three hundred metres above ground, with no net to catch him should he fall. And everywhere he'd gone, he'd imagined the faintest trace of her perfume in the air.

Nothing had stopped him from reaching out for her in the dead of the night, when his guard was at its lowest and all he could feel was *need*. Ferocious, all-consuming need.

Even the air of sadness that hung around her now wasn't enough to make him *not* yearn for her.

His heart kicked into his stomach, knowing it was his fault she wore that look.

Her throat worked to find the words she needed. He forced himself to remain still, to erect a force field against anything she might say.

'Let's end this now, Zaccheo. Divorce me. Surely you'd prefer that to this mockery of a marriage?'

He'd expected it. Hell, her email had left him in no doubt as to her state of mind.

Yet the words punched him in the gut…*hard*. Zaccheo uttered an imprecation that wasn't fit for polite company.

Give her what she wants. Stop this endless misery and be done with it.

It was the selfless thing to do. And if he needed to have learned anything from the stunning, brave woman in front of him, it was selflessness. She'd sacrificed herself for her family and turned over her innermost secrets when she could've just kept quiet and reaped untold wealth. She'd continued to stay under his roof, continued to seek him out, when fear had sent *him* running.

He *needed* to be selfless for her.

But he couldn't. He walked stiffly to the side table and poured a coffee he didn't want.

'There will be no divorce.'

She glared at him. 'You do realise that I don't need your permission?'

He knew that. He'd lived with that fear ever since she'd announced back in Rio that she didn't want to be married to him any more.

'*Sì,*' he replied gruffly. 'You can do whatever you want. The same way I can choose to tie you up in endless red tape for the next twenty years.'

Her mouth dropped open, then she shut her beautiful, pain-filled eyes. 'Why would you do that, Zaccheo?'

'Why indeed?'

She shook her head, and her hair fluttered over her shoulders. 'Surely you can't want this? You deserve a family.'

There it was again. That selflessness that cut him to the core, that forced him to let go, to be a better man. *Dio mio*, but he wanted her to be selfish for once. To claim what she wanted. To claim him!

'How very noble of you to think of me. But I don't need a family.'

Shock widened her eyes. 'What did you say?'

'I don't need a family, *il mio cuore*. I don't need anything, or anyone, if I have you.' *She* was all he wanted. He'd prostrate himself at her feet if that was what it took.

She stared at him for so long, Zaccheo felt as if he'd turned to stone. He knew that any movement would see him shatter into useless pieces.

But he had to take the leap. The same leap she'd taken on the island, when she'd shared something deeply private and heartbreaking with him.

'If you have *me*?'

He risked taking a breath. 'Yes. I love you, Eva. I've been racking my brain for weeks, trying to find a way to make you stay, convince you to stay my wife—'

'You didn't think to just *ask* me?'

'After walking away from you like a coward?' He shook his head. 'You've no idea how many times I picked up the phone, how many times I summoned my pilot to bring me back to you. But I couldn't face the possibility of you saying no.' He gave a hollow laugh. 'Believe it or not, I convinced myself I'd rather spend the rest of my life living in another country but still married to you, than face the prospect of never having even the tiniest piece of you.'

Her face crumbled and he nearly roared in pain. 'That's no life at all, Zaccheo.'

'It was a reason for me to *breathe*. A selfish but *necessary* reason for me to keep functioning, knowing I had a piece of you even if it was your name next to mine on a marriage certificate.'

'Oh, God!' Tears filled her eyes and he cursed. He wanted to take her in his arms. But he had no right. He'd lost all rights when he'd forced her into marriage and then condemned her for trying to protect herself from his monstrous actions.

He clenched his fists against the agony ripping through him. 'But that's no life for you. If you wish for a divorce, then I'll grant you one.'

'What?' Her face lost all colour. She started to reach for him, but faltered. 'Zaccheo…'

A different sort of fear scythed through him as she started to crumple.

'*Eva!*'

By the time he caught her she was unconscious.

Muted voices pulled her back to consciousness. The blinds in the strange room were drawn but there was enough light to work out that she was no longer in Zaccheo's penthouse. The drip in her right arm confirmed her worst fears.

'What…happened?' she croaked.

Shadowy figures turned, and Sophie rushed to her side.

'You fainted. Zaccheo brought you to the hospital,' Sophie said.

'Zaccheo…' Memory rushed back. Zaccheo telling her he loved her. Then telling her he would divorce her…

No!

She tried to sit up.

The nurse stopped her. 'The doctors are running tests. We should have the results back shortly. In the meantime, you're on a rehydrating drip.'

Eva touched her throbbing head, wishing she'd stop talking for a moment so she could—

She stared at her bare fingers in horror. 'Where are my rings?' she cried.

The nurse frowned. 'I don't know.'

'No…please. I need…' She couldn't catch her breath. Or take her eyes off her bare fingers. Had Zaccheo done it so quickly? While she'd been unconscious?

But he'd said he loved her. Did he not love her enough? Tears brimmed her eyes and fell down her cheeks.

'It's okay, I'll go and find out.' The nurse hurried out.

Sophie approached. Eva forced her pain back and looked at her.

'I hope you don't mind me being here? You didn't call when you got back so I assume you don't want to speak to me, but when Zaccheo called—'

Eva shook her head, her thoughts racing, her insides shredding all over again. 'You're my family, Sophie. It may take a while to get back to where we were before, but I don't hate you. I've just been a little…preoccupied.' Her gaze went to the empty doorway. 'Is…Zaccheo still here?'

Sophie smiled wryly. 'He was enraged that you didn't have a team of doctors monitoring your every breath. He went to find the head of the trauma unit.'

Zaccheo walked into the room at that moment, and Sophie

hastily excused herself. The gunmetal shade of his eyes and the self-loathing on his face made Eva's heart thud slowly as she waited for the death blow.

He walked forward like a man facing his worst nightmare.

Just before she'd fainted, she'd told herself she would fight for him, as she'd fought for her sister and father. Seeing the look on his face, she accepted that nothing she did would change things. Her bare fingers spoke their own truth.

'Zaccheo, I know you said…you loved me, but if it's not enough for you—'

Astonishment transformed his face. 'Not enough for *me*?'

'You agreed to divorce me…'

Anguish twisted his face. 'Only because it was what *you* wanted.'

She sucked in a breath when he perched on the edge of the bed. His fingers lightly brushed the back of her hand, over and over, as if he couldn't help himself.

'You know what I did last night before I came home?'

She shook her head.

'I went to see your father. I had no idea where I was headed until I landed on the lawn at Pennington Manor. Somewhere along the line, I entertained the idea that I would sway your feelings if I smoothed my relationship with your father. Instead I asked him for your hand in marriage.'

'You did what?'

He grimaced. 'Our wedding was a pompous exhibition from start to finish. I wanted to show everyone who'd dared to look down on me how high I'd risen.'

Her heart lurched. 'Because of what your mother and stepfather did?'

He sighed. 'I hated my mother for choosing her aristo-crat husband over me. Like you, I didn't understand why it had to be an either-or choice. Why couldn't she love me *and* her husband? Then I began to hate everything he stood for. The need to understand why consumed me. My stepfather was easy to break. Your father was a little more cunning.

He used you. From the moment we met, I couldn't see beyond you. He saw that. I don't know if I'll ever be able to forgive that, but he brought us together.' He breathed deep and shoved a hand through his short hair. 'Possessing you blinded me to what he was doing. And I blamed you for it, right along with him when the blame lay with me and my obsession to get back at you when I should've directed my anger elsewhere.'

'You were trying to understand why you'd been rejected. I tried for years to understand why my father couldn't be satisfied with what he had. Why he pushed his family obsession onto his children. He fought with my mother over it, and it ripped us apart. Everything stopped when she got sick. Perversely, I hoped her illness would change things for the better. For a while it did. But after she died, he reverted to type, and I couldn't take it any more.' She glanced at him. 'Hearing you tell that newspaper tycoon that I was merely a means to an end brought everything back to me.'

Zaccheo shut his eyes in regret. He lifted her hand and pressed it against his cheek. 'He was drunk, prying into my feelings towards you. I was grappling with them myself and said the first idiotic thing that popped into my head. I don't deny that it was probably what I'd been telling myself.'

'But afterwards, when I asked you...'

'I'd just found out about the charges. I knew your father was behind it. You were right there, his flesh and blood, a target for my wrath. I regretted it the moment I said it, but you were gone before I got the chance to take it back.' He brought her hand to his mouth and kissed it, then her palm before laying it over his heart. *'Mi dispiace molto, il mio cuore.'*

His heart beat steady beneath her hand. But her fingers were bare.

'Zaccheo, what you said before I fainted...'

Pain ravaged his face before he nodded solemnly. 'I meant it. I'll let you go if that's what you want. Your happiness means everything to me. Even if it's without me.'

She shook her head. 'No, not that. What you said before.'

He looked deep into her eyes, his gaze steady and true. 'I love you, Eva. More than my life, more than everything I've ever dared to dream of. You helped me redeem my soul when I thought it was lost.'

'You touched mine, made me love deeper, purer. You taught me to take a risk again instead of living in fear of rejection.'

He took a sharp breath. 'Eva, what are you saying?'

'That I love you too. And it tears me apart that I won't be able to give you children—'

His kiss stopped her words. 'Prison was hell, I won't deny it. In my lowest times, I thought having children would be the answer. But you're the only family I need, *amore mio*.'

Zaccheo was rocking her, crooning softly to comfort her when the doctor walked in.

'Right, Mrs Giordano. You'll be happy to hear we've got to the bottom of your fainting spell. There's nothing to worry about besides—'

'Dehydration and the need to eat better?' she asked with a sniff.

'Well, yes, there's that.'

'Okay, I promise I will.'

'I'll make sure she keeps to it,' Zaccheo added with a mock frown. He settled her back in the bed and stood. 'I'll go get the car.'

The doctor shook his head. 'No, I'm afraid you can't leave yet. You need to rest for at least twenty-four hours while we monitor you and make sure everything's fine.'

Zaccheo tensed and caught her hand in his. 'What do you mean? Didn't you say you'd got to the bottom of what ails her?' His eyes met hers, and Eva read the anxiety there.

'Zaccheo…'

'Mr Giordano, no need to panic. The only thing that should ail your wife is a short bout of morning sickness and perhaps a little bed rest towards the end.'

Zaccheo paled and visibly trembled. 'The *end*?'

Eva's heart stopped. 'Doctor, what are you saying?' she whispered.

'I'm saying you're pregnant. With twins.'

EPILOGUE

ZACCHEO EMERGED FROM the bedroom where he'd gone to change his shirt—the second of the day due to his eldest son throwing up on him—to find Eva cross-legged on the floor before the coffee table, their children cradled in her arms as she crooned Italian nursery rhymes she'd insisted he teach her.

On the screen via a video channel, Romeo leaned in closer to get a better look at the babies.

Zaccheo skirted the sofa and sat behind his wife, cradling her and their children in his arms.

'Do you think you'll make it for Christmas?' she asked Romeo. Zaccheo didn't need to lean over to see that his wife was giving his friend her best puppy-dog look.

'*Sì*, I'll do my best to be there tomorrow.'

Eva shook her head. 'That's not good enough, Romeo. I know Brunetti International is a huge company, and you're a super busy tycoon, but it's your godsons' first Christmas. They picked out your present all by themselves. The least you can do is turn up and open it.'

Zaccheo laughed silently and watched his friend squirm until he realised denying his wife anything her heart desired was a futile exercise.

'If that's what you wish, *principessa*, then I'll be there.'

Eva beamed. Zaccheo spread his fingers through her hair, resisting the urge to smother her cheek and mouth in kisses because she thought it made Romeo uncomfortable.

The moment Romeo signed off, Zaccheo claimed his kiss, not lifting his head until he was marginally satisfied.

'What was that for?' she murmured in that dazed voice that was like a drug to his blood.

'Because you're my heart, *dolcezza*. I cannot go long without it. Without you.'

Eva's heart melted as Zaccheo relieved her of their youngest son, Rafa, and tucked his tiny body against his shoulder. Then he held out his hand and helped her up with Carlo, their eldest by four minutes.

Zaccheo pulled them close until they stood in a loose circle, his arms around her. Then, as he'd taken to doing, he started swaying to the soft Christmas carols playing in the background.

Eva closed her eyes to stem the happy tears forming. She'd said a prayer every day of her pregnancy as they'd faced hurdles because of her endometriosis. When the doctors had prescribed bed rest at five months, Zaccheo had immediately stepped back from GWI and handed over the day-to-day running of the company to his new second-in-command.

Their sons had still arrived two weeks early but had both been completely healthy, much to the joy and relief of their parents. Relations were still a little strained with her father and sister, but Oscar doted on his grandsons, and Sophie had fallen in love with her nephews at first sight. But no one loved their gorgeous boys more than Zaccheo. The love and adoration in his eyes when he cradled his sons often made her cry.

And knowing that love ran just as deep for her filled her heart with so much happiness, she feared she would burst from it.

'You've stopped dancing,' he murmured.

She began to sway again, her free hand rising to his chest. She caught sight of her new rings—the engagement ring belonging to his grandmother, which he'd kept but not given her because the circumstances hadn't been right, and the new wedding band he'd let her pick out for their second, family-only wedding—and her thoughts turned pensive. 'I was thinking about your mother.'

Zaccheo tensed slightly. She caressed her hand over his heart until the tension eased out of him. 'What were you thinking?' he asked grudgingly.

'I sent her pictures of the boys yesterday.'

A noise rumbled from Zaccheo's chest. 'She's been asking for one since the day they were born.'

She leaned back and looked into her husband's eyes. 'I know. I also know you've agreed to see her at Easter after my first album comes out.'

Tension remained between mother and son, but when his mother had reached out, Zaccheo hadn't turned her away.

Standing on tiptoe, Eva caressed the stubble she insisted he grow again, and kissed him. 'I'm very proud of you.'

'No, Eva. Everything good in my life is because of *you*.' He sealed her lips with another kiss. A deeper, more demanding kiss.

By mutual agreement, they pulled away and headed for the nursery. After bestowing kisses on their sleeping sons, Zaccheo took her hand and led her to the bedroom.

Their lovemaking was slow, worshipful, with loving words blanketing them as they reached fulfilment and fell asleep in each other's arms.

When midnight and Christmas rolled around, Zaccheo woke her and made love to her all over again. Afterwards, sated and happy, he spread his fingers through her hair and brought her face to his.

'Buon Natale, amore mio,' he said. 'You're the only thing I want under my Christmas tree, from now until eternity.'

'Merry Christmas, Zaccheo. You make my heart sing every day and my soul soar every night. You're everything I ever wished for.'

He touched his forehead to hers and breathed deep. *'Ti amero per sempre, dolcezza mia.'*

* * * * *

Don't miss Romeo's story in
BRUNETTI'S SECRET SON
available December 2015.

MILLS & BOON®
Hardback – November 2015

ROMANCE

A Christmas Vow of Seduction	Maisey Yates
Brazilian's Nine Months' Notice	Susan Stephens
The Sheikh's Christmas Conquest	Sharon Kendrick
Shackled to the Sheikh	Trish Morey
Unwrapping the Castelli Secret	Caitlin Crews
A Marriage Fit for a Sinner	Maya Blake
Larenzo's Christmas Baby	Kate Hewitt
Bought for Her Innocence	Tara Pammi
His Lost-and-Found Bride	Scarlet Wilson
Housekeeper Under the Mistletoe	Cara Colter
Gift-Wrapped in Her Wedding Dress	Kandy Shepherd
The Prince's Christmas Vow	Jennifer Faye
A Touch of Christmas Magic	Scarlet Wilson
Her Christmas Baby Bump	Robin Gianna
Winter Wedding in Vegas	Janice Lynn
One Night Before Christmas	Susan Carlisle
A December to Remember	Sue MacKay
A Father This Christmas?	Louisa Heaton
A Christmas Baby Surprise	Catherine Mann
Courting the Cowboy Boss	Janice Maynard

MILLS & BOON®
Large Print – November 2015

ROMANCE

The Ruthless Greek's Return	Sharon Kendrick
Bound by the Billionaire's Baby	Cathy Williams
Married for Amari's Heir	Maisey Yates
A Taste of Sin	Maggie Cox
Sicilian's Shock Proposal	Carol Marinelli
Vows Made in Secret	Louise Fuller
The Sheikh's Wedding Contract	Andie Brock
A Bride for the Italian Boss	Susan Meier
The Millionaire's True Worth	Rebecca Winters
The Earl's Convenient Wife	Marion Lennox
Vettori's Damsel in Distress	Liz Fielding

HISTORICAL

A Rose for Major Flint	Louise Allen
The Duke's Daring Debutante	Ann Lethbridge
Lord Laughraine's Summer Promise	Elizabeth Beacon
Warrior of Ice	Michelle Willingham
A Wager for the Widow	Elisabeth Hobbes

MEDICAL

Always the Midwife	Alison Roberts
Midwife's Baby Bump	Susanne Hampton
A Kiss to Melt Her Heart	Emily Forbes
Tempted by Her Italian Surgeon	Louisa George
Daring to Date Her Ex	Annie Claydon
The One Man to Heal Her	Meredith Webber

MILLS & BOON®
Hardback – December 2015

ROMANCE

The Price of His Redemption	Carol Marinelli
Back in the Brazilian's Bed	Susan Stephens
The Innocent's Sinful Craving	Sara Craven
Brunetti's Secret Son	Maya Blake
Talos Claims His Virgin	Michelle Smart
Destined for the Desert King	Kate Walker
Ravensdale's Defiant Captive	Melanie Milburne
Caught in His Gilded World	Lucy Ellis
The Best Man & The Wedding Planner	Teresa Carpenter
Proposal at the Winter Ball	Jessica Gilmore
Bodyguard...to Bridegroom?	Nikki Logan
Christmas Kisses with Her Boss	Nina Milne
Playboy Doc's Mistletoe Kiss	Tina Beckett
Her Doctor's Christmas Proposal	Louisa George
From Christmas to Forever?	Marion Lennox
A Mummy to Make Christmas	Susanne Hampton
Miracle Under the Mistletoe	Jennifer Taylor
His Christmas Bride-to-Be	Abigail Gordon
Lone Star Holiday Proposal	Yvonne Lindsay
A Baby for the Boss	Maureen Child